DIRTY BLOOD

THE CRANE DIARIES 2

BY APRYL BAKER

DIRTY BLOOD

Limitless Publishing, LLC
Kailua, HI 96734
www.limitlesspublishing.com

Formatting: Limitless Publishing

ISBN-13: 978-1-64034-491-4
ISBN-10: 1-64034-491-8

DEDICATION

To all the people out there struggling to
feel loved and like you fit in.
Your home is where you choose to make
it and with the people you choose to call
family.
Blood doesn't always make a family.
Love and loyalty make a family.

1

An owl hoots, breaking the silence of the night. I look to the left, to where the sound came from, but all I see is the murkiness of the Louisiana swamp. My biggest concern at the moment is not the ghost I'd agreed to help find, but the alligator or water moccasin that could strike at any minute.

It'll be easy, Cass said. In and out, bag and tag. He never once mentioned we'd be trudging through the swamp. He probably knew I'd balk. Sure, I like the great outdoors as much as anybody, but even I have limits.

I slap at the back of my neck, hoping

I've nailed the mosquito that bit into my flesh. Killing the little suckers gives me a very satisfying sense of revenge.

"You couldn't warn me, could you?" I accuse Cass Willow when he joins me by the tree I've stopped under. I glance up, well aware that snakes can drop from the low hanging limbs.

Cass is one of the hunters I've gotten to know over the last few weeks. I owed him a favor, and he'd decided to call that marker in earlier tonight with a text.

He flashes me a grin, his dirty blond hair falling into those sparking baby blues of his. A dimple appears. My sister Mary calls him charming. I call him just plain old irritating.

"Aww, now, *chèr*, doan be like dat." His thick Cajun accent is just as charming as his smile. It could almost make me forget I have a boyfriend and believe Cass isn't as irritating as he actually is. Almost.

But there is no forgetting Dan Richards. Not for me, not ever.

"Don't be like what?" I snap and round on him. "Don't be irritated and pissed off you have me footing it through the swamp in shoes that are now soaking wet? Don't be mad I'm being eaten alive by mosquitos, or don't be terrified I'm about to be dessert for an alligator?"

"Would you have come if I tol' you where we were goin' ghost huntin'?"

"No."

"Dere you go, Emma. Dat's why I didn't tell you. No one else could come out tonight, and I needed de help. Dis be one bad ghost."

"Tell me more about 'dis bad ghost.'" I can be pissed and still help him. Making me feel needed soothes some of the angry feelings. Not much, but enough so I don't want to strangle him anymore.

"Police got de call late last nigh'. Two dead, and de only survivor tol' dem a strange story." Cass rolls his shoulders, easing some of the tension in them. He's been wary since we stepped into the wooded, swampy area. I get the feeling he doesn't like being here any more than I do. "Dey were out huntin' gators and saw a woman walkin' in de woods. When dey stopped to see if she needed help, she tol' dem she wanted to go home. Like any good Louisiana gent, dey offered to take her home in dere boat."

My father would agree with him. Manners mean a lot to the people in the south, and helping out a woman would top right up there with remembering to call someone ma'am.

"She appeared very thankful and accepted dere offer of help, only once she was in de boat and dey were on der way, she changed."

"Changed?"

Cass looks out over the swamp, his eyes darker than usual. *"Oui, chèr.* Her face went deathly pale, and her eyes went all dark, and dey bled black tears."

"Black eyes?" I interrupt him. "Doesn't that lean more toward demon than ghost?"

His lips tilt in a half-smile. "Can I finish before you go jumpin' to conclusions?"

I shrug. Black eyes mean demons to me, seeing as how I'm part demon. I know a bit more about the subject than Cass, only he's not aware of that little

4

fact. I keep my bloodlines to myself. No need upsetting all the hunters and putting myself in their crosshairs.

"She was dressed all in white, which tells me she could be a White Lady."

"A whatsit?" A sound to my right startles me, and I swing my flashlight in that direction, but the weak beam can't cut through the darkness. I seriously need to outfit myself with a better flashlight.

He shakes his head. "Woman, you really doan know no'tin about de t'ings dat go bump in de night, do you?"

"Considering I spent most of my life ignoring the fact I could see ghosts...then, yeah, I don't know jack about anything. I'm learning, though."

His lips purse. "We need to get you caught up fast, *chèr*. N'awlins is not a place to be unawares. Too many t'ings dat can get de jump on you."

"All I know are ghosts, angels, and demons. Everything else is a mystery to me."

"Den why doan you know wha' a White Lady is?"

"Because to me a ghost is a ghost. I

didn't realize there were different types outside of lost souls and those that go postal because they've been here too long and end up insane."

He looks at me, his eyes assessing. It flips him out I'm Ezekiel Crane's daughter, the biggest bad around these parts, who deals in the supernatural every day, and I'm basically ignorant in that department. I am trying to play catch-up, though. There's so much it gets overwhelming, but I won't give up until I'm armed with all the knowledge I need to protect myself and the people I love.

Cass opens the small backpack he's carried in and pulls out a leather-bound journal, filled with pages of what I assume are notes. He flips until he finds what he's looking for and shows it to me. A sketch of a woman is on the page with every little fact he knows about her. "Remind me to get you one of dese. Dey can be helpful in organizing information."

Not a bad idea. I think I can do better than his scrawl of lines that I wouldn't know was a woman without the title on the page. Drawing is what I do best.

"A White Lady, de Weeping Woman, or de Woman in White, as she's called in many parts of de world, is someone who's suffered a great loss due to tragedy. Dis ghost is most common in rural areas, like de swamp."

"Why does she wear white instead of the clothes she died in?" In my experience, ghosts tend to come to me exactly as they died, in the same clothes, and with every horrible injury they suffered. They can still catch me unawares and scare the devil out of me.

"Doan know, *chèr*. My uncle could tell you. He knows more about dese women den I do."

"Who is our ghost?"

"Doan know dat ei'der." He puts his journal away and slings his backpack over his shoulder. "I didn't have time to do de proper research. I got de call about an hour before I picked you up."

My mouth drops open. "You came in here without knowing anything? Wasn't it you who told me *last week* that research is key?"

"It is," he agrees, "but sometimes we doan have dat luxury."

"This is stupid." I throw my hands up, aggravated. "I may not be the big bad hunter, but I know better than to try to tackle something without any sort of plan. *Do* you have a plan?"

He pulls out his blessed blade, one of the few weapons I know of that can kill a ghost. His isn't a full-on sword, but it's not a dagger either. It falls somewhere in between the two, and he carries it in a sheath attached to his belt and strapped to his leg so it doesn't make any noise when he walks.

"That's your plan? Get close enough to stab her?" When he nods, I let out a sigh. "Then why am I here? I'm a reaper, Cass. My job is to talk a ghost into moving on."

He snorts. "You are som'tin else, Emma Crane. You come face-to-face with a White Lady, talkin' be de last t'ing on your mind. You be runnin' for your life."

"Sometimes it's easier to talk to a ghost than outright murder them. We might be able to save her if we talk to her."

He brandishes his blessed blade. "Dis be all de talkin' I need."

I don't bother replying as I follow him deeper into the heart of the swamp. I need to find this ghost and get us out of here. This place isn't just infested with potential death traps, it's downright creepy. And that means going into reaper mode.

I always imagine my reaping abilities lying dormant at the bottom of an icy cold lake, its water fog-covered. Closing my eyes, I pull up the image of myself walking out and sinking to the bottom. The water closes around me, and I want to fight, to swim to the top as the water tries to drown me. I drowned once, and since then, water scares me. But as Zeke taught me, I have to overcome my fears and let my reaping abilities in, which means letting the water in. Easier said than done.

It takes me a minute, but I stop fighting the sensation of drowning, and white lights swirl up out of the water, surrounding me until I'm wrapped all in that beautiful, cold light of death. I am the cold. I am death.

When I open my eyes, Cass gasps. "Wha' happened to your eyes, girl?"

Mary took a picture of me in reaper mode. My eyes turn the color of a wintery February sky. It's the only thing of hers my true mother left me with. She bound every other ability I have outside of my reaping and the glowy eyes. She was a goddess, and I guess when she used her power, her eyes went that color, or at least that's what Silas told me. Cass has no more idea of who my mother is than he does that Silas, a demon, is my grandfather. Keeping it that way too.

"I'm a reaper, Cass. My eyes reflect that when I reach for my gift."

"It's wicked scary, *mon amie.*"

I know that too, but I'm more interested in getting out of Dodge than I am in his opinions of my reaping.

"Now, be quiet, and let's go find our ghost."

Time to hunt.

The first thing I feel is the essence of hundreds of lost souls. These swamps are full of ghosts and other things that are worse. It's to be expected, though. After Katrina hit, so many lost their lives. They're wailing in pain and grief, confused because no one can hear them. I tune them out. Thanks to the handy dandy tattoo Caleb Malone gave me, ghosts can't overwhelm me anymore. I learned to control my ability enough to focus on one particular ghost at a time, even among hundreds.

"What would this ghost feel like?" I ask Cass, sending my power out ahead of me, searching.

"Angry."

"They're all angry."

He gives me his goofy grin. "Yeah, I guess they are. Lost souls, I'm guessing?"

I nod. "Yeah, lots of hurricane victims, but there are others here as well. Some deaths were accidental, some were gator bait, but some were…" I shudder away from those ghosts. "Some were murdered, and not in an easy way."

"Well, dying's never easy, *chèr*."

"True, but some deaths are easier than others. Now, this ghost we're searching for, can you tell me anything about her other than what the survivor told you? How does a White Lady normally feel?"

"Why does dat matter?" He cocks his head curiously.

"Because ghosts, like humans, are unique. Each one has an energy signature, and if I can find the right frequency, I can find her in this sea of the lost."

"Like lookin' for a needle in a haystack?"

12

"Pretty much."

He goes quiet as we walk. I glance over after a few minutes to see him deep in thought. "I've never t'ought about it like that."

"Most don't." They think of ghosts as hollow impressions left behind, but they're not. It's their essence, their souls. Granted, they don't have the same mojo they did in life unless they've grown really determined or extra angry. Then they can do some real damage. All that anger helps them harness the energy around them and manipulate objects. Or people, for that matter. I've run into a few who could body jump you and take over, my best friend Eric being one of them. He now resides in the body of my ex-boyfriend, Jake Owens.

"So, ghosts are still de people dey were in life?"

I sometimes forget hunters can't see all ghosts like I can. They only see the bad ones, the ones who have so much energy it makes them visible to the living. As a reaper, they're all in my peripheral vision. They can hide, but only for a short time. Eventually, they come to me. My soul is more ghost energy than human, and the light is like a beacon to them.

"Yes. A ghost is a soul trapped here on this plane through no fault of their own. Some don't understand they're dead, others can't accept it, and some are bound here to repeat their deaths over and over. That's where I come in. I help them move on."

"I only see de bad ones. I never t'ought of dem as still bein' de people dey were in life."

"If you're not a reaper, you wouldn't have known."

He grows silent again, thinking over what I told him. Most hunters don't take the time to understand ghosts. They just go in and destroy. By the time they're called in, though, things have usually progressed to the point of no return, and the ghosts are hurting people. I can't blame them for not wanting to get all cozy with them.

The trees thicken overhead, and the weeping willows cling to each other, blotting out the moon. The night is inky black, our flashlights no comfort. It's the kind of deep darkness you only feel at around three in the morning, when the night is quiet, people are asleep, and even the owls are looking for their beds. Usually, I find this time of the night peaceful and soothing, but not tonight. This darkness is eerie.

The farther out my gift reaches, the more anxious I become. Not because of any ghost either. This is different, more potent. It's full of anger and rage, so much so that it's calling to everything supernatural in me.

"Can you feel that?"

"Feel wha'?" Cass stops walking and looks around warily.

"It's more a sense of danger, of something lurking out there, watching us. It's angry. You can't feel that at all?"

"De swamp always has eyes on you. It is de nature of de beast."

"This is different." Cass is human through and through. He may not be sensitive to the same things I am. "I can't explain it, but it's not a ghost. It's something else."

"Dere be lots of things it could be." Cass moves closer to me, his blessed blade held loosely in one hand. I want to inch away from it. I'm still not comfortable around knives. Not after my mother almost killed me with one when I was five. Then the Mrs. Olsen mess…yeah, I don't like knives at all. "Where you feel it comin' from?"

Closing my eyes, I drown out all the ghosts and focus on my unease. My reaping has nothing to do with this, though. Whatever this is, it isn't dead. My demonic heritage woke up recently, so maybe that darkness is drawn to whatever is out here. It's tugging at me, and I start to move forward, aware of only the sweet taste of the darkness lurking.

Ever since I ingested hundreds of wraiths a few weeks ago, the darkness that lives inside me is growing. I haven't told anyone about it, but I'm starting to get worried. It's making me have nightmares and giving me urges to do bad things. Something's been wrong with me since Silas jerked my soul out, and letting all those wraiths in while it was resettling allowed the darkness to take root and grow.

If it doesn't get better soon, I'm going to have to pay a visit to my grandfather.

My skin crawls as we walk deeper into the murky blackness of the swamp. Whatever this thing is, it's out there, watching us, measuring us.

"Careful, *mon amie*," Cass warns. "You're gettin' close to de water."

I reach out blindly for his hand, and he pulls me back onto the path. If I open my eyes, I might break whatever this strange connection is. All thoughts of the White Lady are gone, replaced with the need to know what's out here with me in the dark. Even my fear of being eaten by gators has lessened. This thing calls to me.

The darkness that has been growing inside me for weeks spreads out, using my reaping ability to search for the evil I'm sensing out here. For once, I don't try to beat it back. I let it out, let it search for me. I hate the way it makes me feel. Whenever it comes out to play, my skin gets coated with some kind of metaphysical ick. Black slime. I've seen black slime, thanks to a protection demon sent to kill me by Dan's adoptive mother. Had it leach onto my skin. This is exactly what that felt like.

The scent of bitter chocolate tickles my nose, and I pause. It's so close I can reach out and touch it. Taking several deep breaths, I center myself and look for it, try to taste it. What is this thing?

"Emma," Cass whispers, and the alarm in his voice is enough to interrupt my search.

"What is it?" I open my eyes and look around for anything that could present an imminent threat.

"Doan move."

That's not good.

"Wha…"

He points to our left, keeping his flashlight slightly down.

Glowing yellow eyes stare unblinkingly at us from the shadows. I can't make out the shape because it's partially hidden behind the bushes, but I get the sense that it's bigger than a normal dog. Or maybe not a dog at all. It's standing upright, like a person would.

"Rougarou." The hushed way Cass says its name tells me all I need to know. This thing is beyond dangerous. No clue what it is, but I have no desire to find out.

"Should we run?" I whisper.

He shakes his head. "It's too fast."

"Then what do we do?"

"Fight." His expression tightens, and my belly dives. Uh, I'm not equipped to fight a rooga-whatever. Give me a mugger or even a psychotic killer dead set on doing me harm, and I'm good, but this thing? I don't see it happening. I don't have anything to fight it with either, aside from a pocket knife with an iron blade, a gift from Dan so I would have something to use against a ghost. It's the only thing I'd compromise on. He wanted me to have a full-on knife, but with my aversion to knives, it wasn't something I could do.

"And what am I supposed to do with no weapon?"

"Stay behind me."

Not gonna happen either. Looking

around, I pick up a fallen tree branch that's more of a stout stick. Not the best, but it'll have to do. "Why hasn't it moved?"

"I don't know."

"Have you ever fought one of these things before?"

"No."

"Then how do you know what it is?" I squint, trying to see it better. Maybe it's not a rooga-whatever.

"Because dat's wha' killed my family."

My head snaps back of its own accord. This thing killed his family? Well, maybe not this particular one, but still. I had no idea.

A growl shakes the air around us, and I flinch. That thing is so far past evil, it's not even funny. It's downright scary. Why couldn't I have just followed the ghosts instead of letting my inner darkness dictate we follow the path of something this dangerous?

A visit to Silas is definitely in order.

The bushes rustle, and the thing moves toward us, its eyes intense and full of determination. It is standing upright like a man, but its body is covered in hair, and its ears are pointed like a dog's. The nose, if that's what you could call it, is squished in, the nostrils wide and flared. It's scenting us.

It reminds me of that old wolfman movie from the fifties.

"Is that a werewolf?"

"*Non*, Emma. A werewolf is an entirely different creature. Dis thing, it's de result of a curse. Bad voodoo."

"Voodoo?" I step closer to Cass, eyeing the thing. It's stopped moving, but it's watching us just as closely as we are it.

"*Oui*."

"What's it doing?"

Cass shrugs but tightens his grip on his blade. He doesn't give me or the roogie-thing any warning, just attacks. His lunges forward, blade lashing out, and cuts into the thing's flesh. Smoke sizzles, and a howl rips through the night. Cass goes flying backward. I don't turn to see where he landed, though. The thing is crouched, ready to spring.

Right at me.

"Easy, now," I whisper. "I don't mean you any harm."

Not that the stick in my hand encourages trust, but hey, I'm not throwing it down either.

It cocks its head, listening to me. I think.

"Just leave me and my friend alone, and we'll leave you alone, okay?" I take two hesitant steps backward, and the thing shuffles forward. Not what I intended. It's doglike in appearance, so maybe it behaves the same as a dog? Or wolf, or whatever? Sometimes I have to take a sterner tone with my Hellhound, Peaches, to make her behave.

Would it work for this thing?

"Down, boy." I try to put as much discipline in my voice as I can. "Stay."

Walking backward, it doesn't follow me.

Yes! It worked.

Until it doesn't.

The thing rushes me, and my feet leave the ground with the force of the body that barrels into me. We hit the ground and roll. As soon as the claws sink into my skin, I start screaming unashamedly at the blinding pain. Teeth tear into my shoulder, and I grope blindly for my little pocket knife. Finding it and popping it open even before it's out of my pocket, I take a deep breath then plunge the knife right into what I hope is the neck of the beast.

It merely grunts and bites harder, pulling another scream from me. Where the heck is Cass? Maybe it knocked him unconscious. Either way, I'm the only one who's going to get me out of this.

The stick had fallen long before we landed at the edge of the water. I kick out as hard as I can, but there's no give. I use my little knife to stab it as many times as I can, but still nothing. It's like pinpricks to this thing. My skin tears, and its face comes up, a piece of flesh hanging out of its mouth.

Rage overpowers me, rage like I've only really known once in my life. This thing is killing me, and that means it's killing Dan, the one person I care more about than anyone. His soul is tied to mine, and if I die, so does he. Something opens in my mind, and an energy that had been locked behind a door blazes to life, pouring out of me and hitting the roogie square in the chest. I stand up, my hand going to the wound on my shoulder, and stalk toward the thing, intent on destruction.

"You messed with the wrong girl," I snarl. The creature, which had been stunned, looks at me then flees toward the trees. "Oh, no, you don't!"

Before I can do anything, I hear Cass call out my name. Concern for him outweighs my need for revenge. Turning, I hurry over to where he's lying.

"Ohmygosh!" The words rush out of my mouth as I fall to my knees beside him. He'd landed in such a way that a branch went right through his left thigh.

"Your eyes!" His own go wild, and he tries to get away from me. They have to be black. My demon heritage.

"Never mind my eyes." I pull off the flannel shirt I'm wearing over my tank and use it to make a tourniquet above the wound. Living with Mary and her mom taught me some basic first aid. I have to make sure he doesn't bleed out, and at the same time, try not to move the stick.

"Wha' are you?"

"Someone who's trying to help you." I dig my cell phone out of my pocket and want to scream. "There's no bars!"

"Where…where is de Rougarou?"

"It ran." I have no idea where we are or how to get out of here. Or if that thing is coming back. "How am I gonna get you out of here and to the ER?"

"No time, *chèr*." Cass clears his throat. "We need to go to Miss LaRou's."

"Miss who?"

"Voodoo lady who lives in de swamp. Her home is not far from here."

"I don't think you can walk." Dang it.

Cass pulls his shirt off and tosses it to me. "Best to bandage dat shoulder. You're losing a lot of blood, Emma."

I'd forgotten about the shoulder until he reminded me. The second I look at it, the pain sets in with a vengeance. It slices up and down my body from the many slashes I've endured, as well as the massive bite. This is not good. A wave of dizziness washes over me, and I shake my head to clear it. I don't have time to pass out or to be bashful. Taking off my tank, I plug the wound and attempt to use Cass's shirt to tie it off, but it's no use.

"Come here. I'll do it." His voice is hesitant and six shades of embarrassed, but then again, so am I. If we bleed to death, though, Dan dies, and I can't let that happen. I'd sooner face a Fallen Angel again than let Dan die.

Cass is quick, at least. "Here, help me up. We need to get walkin' before we pass out or de Rougarou comes back."

"What's the difference between that and a werewolf?" I ask to distract us both from the amount of pain we're in as I help him to his feet. He winces and lets out a strangled cry. Why he's trying to be all manly and not show how much pain he's in is beyond me. Every guy I know is like that, though. Just scream and be done with it. He'd feel better.

"A werewolf is created from a disease, lycanthropy. It can be passed through a bite or through genetics. A Rougarou is a man or woman who is cursed to turn into a wolf-like creature for the span of a moon cycle."

"So, this bite…I won't turn into one, will I?"

He shakes his head. "*Non*, but you'll die if we doan kill de Rougarou who bit you."

"That makes no sense. You just said the curse can't be passed through a bite, but it can kill me?"

Cass stumbles, and we both fall. This time he can't stop the scream that tumbles from his lips as the branch slides around in his leg. My scream has nothing to do with his, though.

It has everything to do with the mess of mutilated bodies we've stumbled over and landed on.

I scramble back, dragging Cass with me. We'd found this thing's feeding ground. It must drag all its kills here. Limbs, gore, and the foul smell of body waste curls my nose. I can't even figure out how many bodies there are. There's too many pieces.

"How much farther to this voodoo lady?"

"Too far," Cass murmurs as I help him

back up. "We'd best get movin', Emma."

Casting a glance around us, I waste no more time talking, and we set out as fast as we can.

We make it to the voodoo lady's shack in record time, even limping and woozy from blood loss. Thoughts of Dan keep me going as we struggle with each step. If I die, then so does he. I also know he'll panic when he can't reach me and call my dad. Zeke will send out search parties. Mary knows I'm with Cass and…

"Did you tell anyone where we were going tonight?"

He shakes his head, grimacing. "*Non*. My aunt and uncle drove over to Mobile for a weddin', and my cousins are up north huntin'. I was de only one home when de call came in."

29

"Awesome." Even if Zeke mounts an expedition, he won't know where to look.

Cass shakes his head. "I should have known better den to go huntin' wit'out tellin' anyone. I am sorry, Emma."

"It's okay. You thought we were hunting a ghost. You didn't expect the roogie thingy."

Cass chuckles at my butchering and shortening the name of the creature. "Why do girls always try to nickname t'ings?"

I've noticed the weaker Cass gets, the thicker his accent becomes. When I'd first met him a few weeks ago, it was almost non-existent, but as time passed, he seemed to get more comfortable around me, and that deep Cajun accent came out. It is beyond charming. Tonight, it's so thick I'm having trouble understanding some of what he's saying.

"Is that the place?" I point toward a light up ahead instead of answering him. The house is a shack, a tiny, rundown thing with vines and jars of God only knows what in them sitting on the porch railing.

"Dat be de place, *chèr*." Cass stumbles again, and I catch him. Pain slices through my shoulder, and we both stop for a moment to catch our breaths. "Best get to gettin' on. Dat t'ing could come upon us at any moment."

On that, we are agreed. Ignoring the pain in my shoulder, I tighten my grip around his waist and all but drag him to the shack. Before either of us can place a foot on the porch steps, the door opens, and a woman steps out. She might be forty, or she might be seventy. It's hard to tell. My grandmother is like that. Makes me wonder if it's good genes or something they're both using to slow down the aging process. Given the magic in these parts, I wouldn't put anything past them.

"Cass Willow, wha' you be doing t'inking to bring dat t'ing to my home?"

He cocks his head. "What t'ing?"

"She means me." The way she's giving me the evil eye, she has to mean me.

The woman nods. "She tell you wha' she is?"

Anger begins to simmer in my chest.

She has no right to look at me like I'm something filthy. "What I am doesn't matter right now. What matters is that he has a freaking tree branch embedded in his leg. We need to get him to the hospital. Do you have a landline?"

She eyeballs me for the longest time but finally shifts her attention to Cass. Her lips thin. "Dat is bad, *mon chèr*."

Cass nods, his face even paler here in the glow of the lights from inside her home. He doesn't look good. I'm worried about how much blood he's lost.

"Do you have a phone?" I snap when she doesn't move to help us.

"I do, but no' for the likes of you."

"Fine, but are you willing to let Cass bleed to death? I'm sure his family won't appreciate that."

Cass sags against me, and I bend down, helping him to sit on the porch steps. I loosen the tourniquet for a minute like Mrs. Cross taught me. That's part of why it took us so long to get here. I had to keep stopping to loosen the thing so the blood supply to his lower leg didn't get completely cut off.

Standing back up, I face the hateful woman. "I'm not asking to come into your home or even on the porch, but please, will you call 9-1-1? He needs a hospital."

She hisses at me, and I snarl right back. I swear, if she thinks she's going to scare me after all the crap I've seen, she's got another thing coming. "If you don't help him, I promise you, you *will* be sorry. I will make it my life's work to see to it."

She stomps back in the house and slams the door behind her. Hopefully, she's calling an ambulance.

"Remind me not to get on your bad side, *chèr*." Cass attempts a feeble smile. "You be one scary woman."

I fuss with his leg, ignoring my own wounds. I can feel myself getting woozy again. I've lost a lot of blood too. Can't let him see that, though.

"Right now, I'm one scared woman." I look back toward the darkness, hoping that thing stays away.

"It woan come here." Cass lays a hand on my arm. "Sit, *chèr*. You're hurt too."

"No. I told that woman I wouldn't, and

I won't. Can't have her throwing us both out. How do you know it won't come here?"

He waves to all the weird ropes hanging from the rafters. "De house be warded against it. We're safe for de minute."

The porch door slams open, and the crazy, hateful woman comes back out. "Ambulance is on de way."

"They know how to get here?"

She nods, her eyes straying to all the long gashes on my arms, my legs, my stomach. "You be marked, girl."

Now what nonsense is she going on about?

Cass lets out a gasp. "No."

The woman nods. "The stink is on her. If the beast doan die by her hands, she will suffer and die a horrible death."

She has to be cray-cray, as Mary would say.

"She'll die if we doan get her to a hospital soon enough," Cass says, and all my focus zeroes in on him. Here I thought I'd been playing off how badly I was injured. Guess not.

"It's not that bad." I shift and wince when it tugs on one of the gashes across my stomach, pulling the already torn flesh apart even further. I'd ignored it in lieu of my shoulder because I needed to help Cass walk.

"Emma Crane, you be a worse liar den I am."

"Crane?" The hateful old woman steps even further back, hunching in on the closed door of her house.

"*Oui*, her father be Ezekiel Crane."

The woman's eyes go so dark they blend in with the night sky. "You never said she was a Crane."

"You never bothered to ask my name," I point out snarkily. Can't help it. Sarcasm is like a second skin to me after having grown up in foster care. It can be a better weapon than a knife or a gun. Sarcasm can cut deep and leave a wound long after a physical injury heals.

Her face pales, and she rushes back inside.

"What is that all about?"

"Most here in de bayou, dey are afraid of Ezekiel Crane."

35

Yes, my father is a very bad man who has done very bad things. It always strikes me as odd when I see the fear he inspires in others. He's not like that with me; he's just my dad who loves me.

When she comes back out, she's carrying what I'm thinking are bandages and all sorts of little bottles with liquid in them. "What's that?"

"I can't have you bleeding out on my porch. Your papa would not like it."

So, she hears my dad's name, and she's willing to help me now? I want to snort, but I'm too woozy. The dizziness I've been fighting off for a while chooses now to decide to overwhelm me, and I stagger where I stand. My vision's getting blurry too. I can't pass out. Not until I know we're safe. I won't.

"Cass, I think you better move," I whisper as I sway.

"Why?"

"Because I'm about to fall, and I don't want to hurt your leg."

His eyes widen, and he barely has time to scoot before I'm falling. I must have lost more blood than I thought. Did the moon disappear behind the clouds? It seems darker.

"You will not be dyin' on my land today, *chèr*!" The hateful woman rushes over and forces some kind of liquid into my mouth. It's the nastiest thing I've ever tasted. She holds my mouth and nose closed until I swallow.

"Oh, no, you doan." Cass's angry words reach my fuzzy mind. I don't know what he's going on about, but I blink and try to focus on him. He's staring at the voodoo lady with open hostility. "You touch her hair or her blood, and it woan just be her papa you have to worry about."

She was trying to get my blood? That's not good. It's one of the first things I learned from Zeke. Never let anyone near your blood or hair or something that belongs to you. It can give them power over you and be used in spells and potions against you. Especially here in the bayou of Louisiana.

My gaze swivels to hers. She's holding a bloody rag, one she'd pressed against the wounds on my legs. "Drop it."

I don't recognize the sound of my voice. It's deeper, harsher, and full of something dark and deadly. She drops it and backs away. I pick up the bottle of water and toss it to her. "Wash your hands."

She picks it up slowly, and I note that there is blood on her dress. "Strip."

"What?" She looks up from her bent position, midway from picking up the water.

"My blood is on your dress. Strip."

Her nostrils flare, and even Cass looks worried. I don't know that much about voodoo, but once you face a Fallen Angel, nothing has the power to really scare you to the depths of your soul. She may have all these people out here terrified of her, but not me.

When she doesn't move fast enough, I'm up, and some of the fuzziness has cleared. The darkness inside has crept closer to the surface, and when her face pales, I know my eyes have gone black. That's part of the reason I have this newfound strength. The demonic side is taking over, and when it does, my human body isn't nearly as fragile as it usually is. Oh, I can still suffer horrible damage, don't get me wrong, but my body will function like I've only been scratched. One of the perks of being part demon.

"Wha' are you?"

"You really don't want to find out, *chèr*." I stress the endearment, not even attempting to conceal my contempt for her.

"She's magnificent, isn't she?"

Everyone but me jumps at the sound of Silas's voice. I hadn't expected him to show up, but I'm not surprised. He can always find me when no one else can. If Zeke and Dan were panicking, then the obvious choice was summoning the demon.

"Be gone, demon!" The hateful woman snarls at him and starts to mutter something.

"No." Without even moving, I imagine her mouth closed and unable to speak, and it just happens. It scares me a little, but Silas grins like the Cheshire cat.

Silas pushes off from the tree he's leaning against and walks over to where

I'm standing. "You're a mess, my darling girl."

"Yeah, well, it's been a night."

"I can see that." He leans in and sniffs before shaking his head. "Honestly, girl. Every time I see you, you're in need of even more protection. How did you get tangled up with a Rougarou?"

"It wasn't by choice." He looks tired. I wonder what he was up to before he came to find me. Nothing good. He stinks of sulphur, and it's only ever this strong when he's been up to no good, like making deals.

He raises a perfectly arched brow, his eyes intrigued. Silas typically keeps his human form. I don't know if this is what he always looked like or if the very British gentlemen is just who he chooses to be. He's a beautiful man, and that makes me even more wary of him. Beauty often hides the darkest of hearts. Silas is my grandfather, and he loves me in his own way, but that doesn't mean he won't hurt me to get what he wants. He's done it before, and I have no doubt he'd do it again. He might regret having to, but that wouldn't stop him.

"Cass and I were looking for a ghost that ripped into some people and found the roogie thingy instead."

His eyebrows shoot up. "Roogie?"

"I can't remember the name, so it's a roogie."

He shakes his head. "The things you do, Emma Rose."

I feel the darkness begin to retreat, and my legs start to shake. Silas catches me before I fall. He lays me out next to Cass, who's shoved so far back against the porch railing, it's not even funny.

He then turns his attention to the voodoo lady, who looks more terrified than anyone I've ever seen. Silas scares her more than I do.

"Is the blood on her dress yours, my darling girl?"

I nod, the dizziness rushing back. Downside to being part demon? When that side retreats, all the effects of the human injuries return.

Silas stalks over and rips it off her. She lets out a muted sound because her lips don't open. Picking up the abandoned bottle of water, he douses her in it, making sure to wash off every drop of my blood. He even checks her over to make sure she's not holding any of my hair or ripped skin. Silas is thorough, if nothing else.

"Into the house with you, witch, and do not come back out." He mutters something, and her mouth opens. She rushes inside, and I hear the deadbolt slide into place.

"Do you know her?" I ask when Silas squats in front of me to start checking my wounds.

"Possibly. I've met many witches in my day." He frowns. "I cannot heal these."

"Why not?"

"Because they were made by the Rougarou, and the sickness is transferred to you. Those wounds woan heal until you kill the beast."

Cass has lost a lot of his Cajun accent. He does that around new people. I don't know why. I need to chat with him about that.

"You didn't escape either." Silas points

to the claw marks on Cass's arm. How had I missed those? "His stink is on you too, boy."

Cass's nostrils flare. He doesn't like to be called a child any more than I do.

The wail of sirens sounds in the distance. I'm not sure how far the ambulance can come, as we walked into the swamp, but I'm hoping we can get out of here sooner rather than later.

"Will you go let Zeke know we're on our way to the hospital?"

He frowns. "I'm not so sure I should leave you, Emma Rose. You're very close to bleeding out."

"You just said you can't do anything to heal them," I point out. "And you know Zeke. He's going out of his mind, and Dan…"

"Yes, Daniel." Silas frowns. "He was the one who summoned me."

"Dan did?" Wow. Dan hates Silas.

"That is how I knew something was seriously wrong. The boy would rather suffer a horrible death than call on me for help. I like him, my darling girl. You need to keep that one."

43

"The police and the ambulance are almost here, Silas. Please take all the bloody rags so she can't get them and go. That is unless you want to explain to the police what you're doing here?"

He shakes his head. "As you wish, but if you have need of me, just call my name. I will hear you." And with that, he's gone. Just poofs away.

Cass is quiet while we wait for the ambulance to make its way to us. I know he has questions, but I'm not in the mood to answer them. I've come to count on Cass as a friend, and I know the hunter in him will never be friends with someone who is part demon. I don't want to face that yet, so I don't even try to talk.

By the time we're loaded up in the ambulance, it's all I can do to stay conscious. I only hope I don't die between the swamp and the hospital.

If I die, Dan dies.

Please, God, I pray, *please don't let me kill him.*

The sound of machines beeping is the first thing I hear when I wake up. It's a sound I've grown accustomed to over the years. I think I've spent more time in hospitals than I have in actual homes since I was eleven. I was always getting hurt as a kid because I was a tomboy who never backed down from a fight. I never fought fair either. I'd use whatever I had to in order to win. And I never lost a fight.

I'm still really woozy. I blink open bleary eyes and shut them just as quickly when the room decides to tilt and torture me. I must have lost a lot of blood.

"She's waking up."

Dan. His voice is calming, and some of my anxiety melts away at the sound, but how is he here?

Trying to force my vision to calm down, I open my eyes again, but...nope. Unless I want to hurl all over Dan and whoever else is beside the bed, that's probably not a good idea.

"Don't move too much, *ma petite*." My father, Ezekiel Crane, sounds as worried as he did when I almost died from seizures. I must be in pretty bad shape. "You're still recovering from massive blood loss. The doctors are amazed you survived."

"I'm stubborn like that." My voice is raspy. "Dan? Are you okay?"

"I'm fine." His hand slips around mine. "You scared me. I thought we were both goners there for a bit."

"It takes more than a swamp creature to take me out." And I'd never forgive myself if I did that to Dan. He means too much to me.

"She's a Crane." The arrogance in Zeke's voice makes me snort, but then I wince when the sound and movement ricochet through my head.

"What is it?" Zeke asks. Ever since my headaches came back last month, he's been worrying himself to death.

"Just a headache, Papa. It's nothing to be concerned about."

I don't have to open my eyes to imagine the way his face will have tightened and his lips thinned. He won't let this go.

"They will do a scan." I hear his footsteps retreating.

"Dan?"

"Yeah, babe?" A tiny thrill goes through me every time he calls me babe or baby. I know a lot of women wouldn't like it; I know some who don't. They think it transfers them back to the age when women's rights were dependent upon men. I personally don't see it that way. It's just a term of endearment that I adore.

"Who else is in here?"

"No one. It's just you and me." His lips graze my hand, and a shiver goes through me.

"We almost died."

"I know. I was at home having a family dinner when it started. I think I nearly gave my brother a heart attack. Cam knows about the supernatural, he knows my life is tied to yours, but he'd never seen what happens when that link between us is in danger."

"I bet your mother hates me even more."

When he doesn't say anything, I know I've hit the nail on the head. "Think she'll ever like me?"

"It doesn't matter, Mattie. I like you, and that's all that counts."

He also refuses to call me Emma. I was Mattie Hathaway when he met me, and I'll be Mattie until the day we die.

"How did you get here so fast?"

"Squirt, you've been unconscious for almost a full day."

"What?" I try to sit up, and he pushes me back down.

"Uh-uh. You're dizzy. I know this because I'm a little dizzy. Sitting up will only make it worse."

"Cass?"

"He's fine, albeit a little cranky. He may be getting sprung soon, though. They only kept him overnight to make sure he got enough antibiotics in his system to fight any infection. He came by to check on you, but he didn't stay long. I think your dad intimidates him."

"Zeke intimidates everyone."

"True."

We sit quietly, his thumb rubbing back and forth along my knuckles. He's humming, a habit I noticed when we'd all come to New Orleans a year ago. He has a nice singing voice too. He sang for me once, but he doesn't like to do it often. I think he's bashful. It's cute.

"Cass is going to have questions," I say after a bit. "He may have seen me with black eyes. I can't remember. A lot of last night is fuzzy."

"Well, he'll either understand or he won't, but either way, I'll make it clear to him you are not something to be hunted."

The steel in his words sends another little shiver through me. Since the Angel gave him the Sword of Truth, Dan has changed. He's grown up a lot, both physically and mentally. He was tall to begin with, but over the last year, he's grown to a towering six-foot-five. I'm five-three. He's a good foot taller than I am. He's also filled out, and the man has some serious muscle going on. He's become a true warrior of the Swords.

"Soooo…."

"So?" he prompts when I don't finish.

"Silas, huh?"

He chuckles, but there is no mirth in it. "He could get to you faster than anyone else. Summoning a demon in front of the family was not ideal, though."

I groan. "Your brother probably hates me as much as your mom now, huh?"

"Actually, no."

I squint, and when the world doesn't spin too much, I open my eyes the barest fraction to see him grinning down at me. "No?"

"Nope, he's grateful to you for saving my life. Once he understood what you did, he went from blaming you for bringing Mom's offenses to light, to being thankful you loved me enough to save me."

Huh. The one time I'd met Cameron had been at the Charlotte Police Department the day everyone had been hauled in for questioning in the matter of the death of Amelia Malone, Dan's birth mother. Ann Richards had murdered his mother and taken him for her own. Granted, she thought she was saving him from evil, when that couldn't have been farther from the truth. The Malones saved people from evil, not brought it into their lives. Not that his mom will ever admit that, though.

"What Cam *doesn't* like is the fact that his son is now fascinated with a demon."

"Silas?"

"Yeah, his vanishing act charmed my nephew. I tried to explain to Bran that Silas wasn't a good person, that he was evil. His response? Then why are you asking him to find your girlfriend?" Dan shakes his head, and a real smile tips up the corners of his mouth. "He had me there."

"He sounds like a smart cookie, just like his uncle."

"He's a little nightmare." Fondness

dispels the aggravated look. "The kid is killer on the football field, even at ten. Tells us he wants to be an NFL player when he grows up."

"I bet your dad is ecstatic." Earl Richards was born and raised in football. The fact his grandson inherited his love of the sport has to have made his year.

"Yeah. You'd think me and Cam were invisible when Dad and the kid start talking football."

I laugh and wince. Now, that one hurt. More than hurt. It drove through my skull like a jackknife.

"Mattie, why didn't you tell me your headaches were back?" Dan doesn't sound mad, but I know him. He's mad.

"Because you'd have worried, and you have more than enough of that to go around with your mom's trial coming up." I know he felt some of the headaches, but he doesn't feel them as much as I do. It's more like a nagging headache than the pounding ones I get. All thanks to Silas. He devised a tattoo to help mute the minor stuff when it comes to what Dan experiences. Silas agreed with Dan in that he needed to know when I was truly hurt and refused to mute everything like I wanted.

He sighs. "Mattie Louise Hathaway Crane. Don't you dare try to hide your pain from me. How can I be in it for the long haul when you go out of your way to conceal things from me? We've got to trust each other for this to work, Squirt. I think we've both been lied to enough to last us ten lifetimes, don't you?"

"I didn't lie."

"You think omitting the truth isn't lying? Pot, kettle, black?"

He had to bring that up, didn't he? Back when I found out about him and Meg dating, I told him omitting the truth was still a form of lying. Dang it. I hate when he throws my own logic back at me.

"Had to go there, didn't you?"

He grins lazily, but it doesn't wash away the concern. Those big brown puppy dog eyes are already working their magic. I can never lie to him when he looks at me like that. I just blurt things out. It's very aggravating.

"No more hiding things from me."

"But…"

He puts a finger against my lips. "I will tell your father."

I gasp. "You wouldn't dare!"

"Try me."

And the warrior is back, the sword blazing where it's strapped to his back. Most of the time, even I can't see it, but when he's getting all righteous, it flares to life. It's so bright it hurts the eyes to look at. Maybe that's what I am to ghosts. Zeke always tells me I'm so full of ghost energy, I'm like a shiny beacon in the dark they can't ignore.

"Fine."

He leans down and kisses my forehead. "Thank you."

Zeke walks back in with who I assume is the doctor arguing about a CT scan. I roll my eyes. I don't need a CT scan. This pain isn't like last time. It's close, but I'm not there yet. Granted, the headaches really flared up when my demonic side woke up last month, but I told neither Dan nor Zeke about that little fact.

"Mr. Crane, I understand her history, but the fact is she's being treated for wounds caused by a wild animal and blood loss. She hasn't shown the need for a CT scan."

"She's having headaches again." My dad's voice has gone cold as ice. "Either you do the scan, or I call the hospital administrator and discuss your lack of concern for my daughter."

"Papa." I don't hide the censure in that one little word.

"Don't give me that tone, young lady!" He wags his finger at me. "Not after almost losing you to seizures last year. I won't stand for it."

The doctor ignores him and comes over to me. "Hello, there, Miss Crane. You gave us all quite a scare. How are you feeling?"

"Dizzy, my eyes hurt, and I think I might hurl at any second."

"That would fit with the amount of blood you lost. We're still quite concerned about infection, so we're giving you high doses of antibiotics."

Sounds about right.

"Now, *are* you having headaches?"

"Yeah. I have a really nasty one right now."

"Are they like the ones you experienced before?"

"This one is pretty close. The others weren't so bad, but they're getting that way."

That draws accusatory glares from both Zeke and Dan.

"Then we'll run a few tests to ease everyone's fears." He makes a note on his tablet, which I assume is my chart, before he leaves. Everything is digital these days.

Zeke's lips work soundlessly. He's torn between yelling at me and trying not to because he's afraid. It's hilarious, and if my head wasn't killing me, I'd laugh. Dan, however, has no such concerns.

"What did you do?"

"Hmm?" I try to play it off.

"Uh-uh." He leans down until his forehead is pressed against mine. "What. Did. You. Do?"

Crap. That sword is back to blazing, and my dad lets out a gasp.

"What de…"

Dan ignores Cass's startled half-question. He's got eyes only for me.

"I asked Silas to make sure the little stuff didn't bother you."

He lets out a strangled breath and takes several steps away from me. He's not just mad. He's furious. I've never seen Dan look at me like this before, with so much rage in his eyes.

"Emma Rose." Disappointment flares in my father's eyes, and I look away, anywhere but at the two men who love me more than their own lives. I was only trying to protect Dan…well, no. Best to be honest. I didn't want him running or texting every single time he got some weird feeling. I was serious when I told him I wanted to be me without him. Sometimes a girl just has to face her own problems without her man running in to save the day. I'm a strong woman who can handle herself.

Ignoring them both, I turn my attention to Cass, who's sitting in a wheelchair being pushed by his cousin, Robert Willow. They share the same dirty blond hair, but Robert's build is wider than Cass's. I remember Cass telling me his family died. Did Robert's parents take him in?

"Hey, you. I see you survived the attack of the tree branches."

His lips twitch, but he tries to hide it. "I see you're finally awake, *chèr*."

That beautiful, charming Cajun accent is muted. I need to ask him why he hides it so much, especially around strangers.

"I am, but I think I'd rather go back to being asleep." I cast a meaningful glance at Dan, who's pacing, clenching and unclenching his hands. He's beyond pissed.

Cass looks at him, squinting. "I thought I saw…"

"A sword strapped to his back?" I ask.

He nods, frowning at Dan.

"You did. He carries The Sword of Truth."

"That's real?" Robert blurts out.

"Very much so." I sigh. "How you feeling, Cass?"

"Like a tree attacked me?" He nudges Robert to wheel him closer to the bed.

"Why don't you go see what's keeping Caryle? You remember the last time she got turned loose in a gift shop?"

Robert rolls his eyes. "We're banned from all of LAX's gift shops."

"*Oui.*' A smile curves Cass's lips. "Best to go get our girl."

Robert nods. "Glad you're all patched up, Emma."

"Me too."

His eyes stray to my father. I know he's unsure about leaving Cass with the infamous Ezekiel Crane.

"I'll keep him safe."

Robert snorts. He knows as well as I do that I'm in no shape to do anyone any good, but then again, he doesn't know my dad like I do. He won't do anything to Cass.

"Go on. Find Caryle before security calls looking for you." Cass pushes him a little, and Robert finally gives in. Only when he's gone does Cass turn back to me. "I got some questions, *chèr.*"

"Figured you did, but I don't think now is the time." Both Zeke and Dan are too pissed to deal with a rational discussion on why I might be next on the hunter's hit list.

"No." Dan cuts off whatever Cass is about to say. "I think now is the perfect time." He comes over to sit beside me, gently moving me so he can pull me into his lap. His arms go around me, and I settle back, leaning against his chest. Since Dan technically died, he's a lot colder than he used to be. He was a furnace at one point, but now his temperature runs on the cooler side. Not that it bothers me. I'm always cold.

"We need to talk about your eyes, Emma."

"What about them?" Zeke has moved closer, staring down at Cass, daring him to say anything.

"Dey were black, Emma."

Crap on toast. He had seen that. I'd hoped against hope he hadn't.

"Yeah, they tend to do that when I get pissed sometimes."

He frowns. "*Non, chèr*. Dey were demon black."

Again, I merely nod.

"She's part demon." Dan's arms

tighten when he lets that truth slip between his lips. I want to kick him. I wasn't going to tell Cass. I was gonna lie through my teeth. "And she is not to be hunted."

Cass looks shell-shocked, his eyes blown wide. I know it's a lot to take in. When Eli found out, he walked away from me. Left me. It hurt in a way I didn't realize it could. The one thing that came out of all that pain was the man sitting beneath me. He didn't leave. Not once. Officer Daniel Richards truly *is* in it for the long haul, half-demon and all. He doesn't care my grandfather is a demon. He loves me despite all that.

"I…" Cass clears his throat, clearly thrown. I don't think he was expecting that or Dan's forthright way of just putting it out there. Neither was I, for that matter, but leave it to Mr. By the Book to state it matter-of-factly. "You're a demon?"

"Part demon." I hold onto Dan's hand like it's the last lifeline left in a sea of killer whales. "My great something-or-other grandfather was a demon. I inherited some of those qualities. I can usually keep it under control, but when someone I love is threatened, it flares to life."

"Someone you love?" Cass cocks his head curiously.

"Dan's soul is tied to mine. If one of us dies, so does the other," I explain. "When someone or something threatens him, there's this rage that wakes up. I can't control it, and honestly, if it means I can protect him, I don't want to. That rage gives me strength, and if that means my eyes go black and I become a little less human, I'm okay with it."

"I'm not," Dan snarls. His breath tickles my ear, and it sets off another shiver, this one a mix of desire and uneasiness. He and I never really talked about what my being half-demon means. I think maybe we need to have that conversation sooner rather than later.

"Dan…"

"No," he cuts me off, "you are the kindest, gentlest person I've ever met, Squirt. If that goes away because you're trying to protect me, then that's not good.

I won't let the darkness in you eat you alive from the inside out. Not because of me."

Yeah, definitely sooner rather than later.

"He's right, Emma Rose." Zeke drops down into the chair Dan vacated earlier. "I don't want you to lose the goodness in you. Letting that darkness out...it's something you can't take back, and it changes you."

I've grown used to the shadows that haunt my father's eyes. They darkened just now, and I wonder what kind of experience he's speaking from.

"I did not know about our family's ties to demon bloodlines until you told me, but knowing that now, I understand some of the choices I made in my youth, choices I can't take back. If we can control the darkness from stealing around your soul, we need to. I don't want you to look back on your youth and regret the decisions you made because the darkness hammered at you and warped your thought process."

Wow. Was that my dad admitting he

did bad things he regrets? He's usually very arrogant about it and not the least remorseful. I wonder what choices he had to make that cause those shadows in his eyes.

Even Cass looks awed at the great Ezekiel Crane admitting regret.

I look up at Dan, and his brown eyes are like warm, gooey chocolate. "Promise me, Mattie. Promise no more hiding things from me."

"The headaches started when my demonic side woke back up."

I slap a hand over my mouth. What the…I did not mean to say that.

Dan and his danged puppy dog eyes.

He lets out a shaky breath. "Well, we know that while you have supernatural powers, your body is very much human. It's not meant to contain everything you can do. That's what happened last time. It makes sense they'd start back up, but hiding that? That's a no go. You will undo whatever you did so I can't feel it."

"Nope, not gonna happen. You don't need to feel it if I get a splinter. Besides, Silas only muted the little stuff, not the life-threatening stuff. He refused."

"He knows if he did that and you got hurt, he wouldn't be breathing anymore." The quiet truth in Dan's voice is enough to make even Cass shiver. Dan is a lot scarier than he used to be. "And the headaches are not little stuff, and especially not if they're getting worse."

"Can we deal with that later?" I implore. "We need to answer Cass's questions before Robert and Caryle get back."

"As much as I want to yell, *ma petite* has a point. The hunter must be dealt with."

When Cass's eyes widen, I shoot my dad a glare. Zeke did that on purpose just to scare him.

"What he means is we need to answer your questions. He's not going to hurt you. I promise."

Cass does not look convinced, not that I blame him. If Zeke wasn't my father, I might be a little afraid of him too. I wouldn't show it, but on the inside, I'd be quaking in my proverbial boots.

"She's still the same person you've

gotten to know." Dan's chin rests on the top of my head, and I shift, trying to get comfortable. I pull my shoulder a little too hard and hiss at the pain. I'd forgotten the thing took a bite out of my shoulder. My stomach wounds have been aching since Dan picked me up and put me in his lap, but not enough to make me move.

"Do you need more pain meds?" Zeke's concern drowns out his anger.

"No more drugs. You know how I feel about them." Growing up in foster care, I'd seen what happened when kids got hooked on prescription drugs. It could be worse than a heroin addiction. And my mom was a heroin addict. I do my best to stay away from the stuff.

Zeke looks ready to argue, but Dan nods. "How about we ask the nurse for some Motrin instead?"

"That'll work." Ibuprofen, I'll do, but anything more than that, I'm not willing to accept.

Zeke gets up to go find a nurse and harass her until she brings me some meds. The relief on Cass's face is palpable.

"I get it," Dan tells him once the door is closed. "Here's this person you've gotten to know and trust, and then you learn something that goes against everything you've ever been taught. You wonder if it makes her different, if she's still the same person, or if she's hiding something behind the mask she shows you."

Cass cocks his head, listening, but then so am I. I've never head Dan talk about me like this before.

"Before I met her, everything was black and white to me. If I couldn't see it or touch it, it wasn't real. The supernatural? A show on TV. Horror movies were something I took girls to so they'd jump and cling to me."

Really? He had to add that part in, didn't he?

"But then I met this girl who looked so scared, I knew I had to help her. She was tough as nails and a smartass."

"Hey!" I elbow him and wish I hadn't when pain shoots all the way down my arm.

"Easy, there, Rocky. You're going to hurt yourself." He rubs my arm, and it's then I notice the bandages. Both my arms are covered in bandages. "Anyway, I got to know her and discovered she was hiding behind that tough exterior. She's kind and gentle, loyal to a fault, and will bend over backward for the people she loves. I thought she was a little crazy at first, telling me she could see ghosts."

"You ignored me for three days," I point out.

Dan laughs. "No, not so much ignoring you as wrapping my head around the fact that you believed what you were saying. Took me a bit, but there was something about her, something I couldn't ignore. I wanted to help her. Getting to know her, learning what she could do wasn't just real, but that I had the same kind of paranormal heritage she did, it threw me. In all honesty, I thought about walking away, regaining some semblance of my life, but I couldn't. I couldn't walk away from her. I'd sooner quit breathing than do that. I was all in, even though I didn't fully understand my feelings. Learning that her great something-or-other grandfather was a demon didn't change who she was. She was still the same girl who held my heart hostage. We can't change who our family is, but we can be better than how other people choose to define us. Even Silas knows she's better than any of us, including him. He actively works to keep her safe."

"He's the demon who came to find us last night?"

I nod. "He's my grandfather."

Cass swallows. "I...I doan know wha' to say."

"Don't say anything right now." Dan lips graze my temple. "Think about it. Think about Mattie and everything you know about her, how she leaps to put herself in danger to protect those who can't. Does that sound like a demon who's only out for themselves?"

"She isn't any'tin like I expected."

Dan smiles. "No, she's not. She's so much *more*."

The things this man says. He's going to ruin me.

"But I will warn you. If you think for a

moment I will let you hunt her, you are dead wrong. If any harm comes to her at the hands of any hunter, I know who to come looking for. And trust me when I tell you, if you hurt her, or cause her any harm, you won't be breathing come morning." He doesn't have to add in the dead or not part. It's pretty clear what he means. If I go down, so does Dan, but that won't prevent him from coming after Cass.

Cass stares him down then nods. "I understand."

I hope so, because I don't want to be a target any more than I already am. We settle into a tense silence until Robert comes and wheels Cass away.

I'm left with a sick feeling in the pit of my stomach.

I really hope Dan got through to him.

"Hathaway, I thought we agreed no more hospitals."

Eric throws the blinds open, and I squint when the bright sunlight assaults my eyes. He's holding a cup of coffee in one hand and running the other through his short brown hair. Blue eyes peek at me from underneath lashes long enough to make a woman envious. Mischief plays in their depths, reminding me he's always up to something.

Dan yawns and stretches in the chair. The nurses ran him out of my bed toward dawn. I missed him the second he left my side, and sleep eluded me. He drifted off, but ghosts kept popping in and disturbing me. It's not an easy thing to wake up and see an old woman with tufts of hair clinging to her head, her body skin and bones from the cancer that had eroded everything that made her who she was. Milky eyes completed her creepy factor. I'd screamed my head off, not expecting it. That was the beginning of the parade of souls in and out of my room last night. Can't really put up a salt barrier either. How would we explain that one to the staff?

Mary waltzes into the room carrying a drink tray full of coffee and a Hardee's bag. The smell of greasy fast food breakfast tickles my nose, and my stomach growls loudly in appreciation. Mary, Dan, and Eric all laugh at me. As long as she hands over that bag, she can laugh all day at my stomach's need to express itself.

"What happens when you get old and that metabolism of yours slows down?" Mary's long blonde hair is done up in some kind of elaborate braid. She's been into YouTube fashion channels lately, and it's starting to rub off on her. Her makeup and hair are almost always perfect. My grandmother has even been hinting at me to watch a few of them. I don't really care about hair or clothes, though. I'm just me, and you either accept me as I am, or you don't. Not that my grandmother doesn't, but sometimes I get the feeling she'd enjoy a granddaughter who loves shopping, clothes, and makeup. But I am who I am.

"Then I'll get fat and be happy." I take the bag she holds out and open it, inhaling the scent of sausage and eggs. "I love you, Mary."

Mary smiles and starts handing out coffee. It's not from Hardee's, but the coffee shop down the street from our dorm room on the Tulane campus. Best coffee ever. Well, more of a latte than a coffee for me. I sip at the foamy goodness the second it's in my hand.

"Careful," Dan warns, accepting his from Mary with a nod of thanks. "You haven't had anything to eat on top of those meds yet."

"They're pumping it into my IV," I

dismiss. I'm starving. I pull out the first biscuit and hand it over to Dan then drag out the second. A chicken biscuit. Toss that one to Eric. The third one is the bacon, egg, and cheese. My personal favorite. The last one has to be Mary's, so she gets the bag.

"Slow down." Mary laughs when I shove the first bite into my mouth. "I can bring you more. Geez, if I had known you were this hungry, I would have brought you two…no, three."

"Wow, Hathaway, I had no idea you could eat so fast."

I look down, and to my astonishment, the biscuit has disappeared in the time it's taken everyone else to unwrap theirs. I really am hungry, I guess. My belly groans in protest when it realizes no more will be coming.

"Uh, Em…" Mary is frowning, staring from me to her biscuit. "Do you want this one too?"

"Please?" I hold out my hand, my stomach cramping from hunger.

"Dat is no' good, *chèr*."

We all jump at the sound of Cass's

voice. Dan sits up straighter, remembering our little talk last night. Cass is alone this time, so I'm guessing he came to talk.

"What's not good?" Eric goes over and holds the door open a little wider so Cass can wheel himself in.

"De hunger." Cass's own stomach growls in response to the yummy smells. "Doan feed de beast."

"Beast?" I gasp. "I am not a beast, I'm just starving."

"*Non*, Emma. It is *de* beast. It's de curse of de Rougarou."

"I don't understand."

"Our blood is poisoned with de sickness, and it's making us starved. De more we eat, the faster our minds will give in to de curse."

"Explain." The bite in Dan's tone is downright scary. Mary and Eric both glance at him, shocked.

"The roogie that attacked us?"

"Roogie?" Mary frowns. "What's a roogie?"

"*Non*, no' a roogie." Cass rolls his eyes, exasperated. "A Rougarou."

"Okay, what's a Rougarou, then?"

"It's a curse. Kinda like a werewolf, but not a real werewolf," I explain. "But it makes no sense to me. If you turn into a wolf, you're a werewolf, right?"

"That sounds right," Eric agrees.

"*Non, chèr.*" Cass shakes his head. "I tried to explain last night, but we got sidetracked."

Dan's usually warm brown eyes are ice cold. He leans back in his chair, propping his feet up on the hospital bed, and adopts what I call the patented Officer Dan look. He looks bored, but I know that's when he's paying the most attention. It's a look I've tried to duplicate and failed at more times than I care to count.

"Werewolves are a whole other beast, as are shifters."

"What's the difference?" Mary asks, sitting down in the only other chair in the room, leaving Eric to lean against the wall.

Cass sighs and runs a hand through his hair. "I did no' expect to be givin' a huntin' 101 class dis mornin'."

76

"Are there classes?" Eric blows into his coffee to cool it before taking a drink.

"*Non.*"

"Well, there should be," Mary declares. "Might save a few lives."

He smiles sadly. "You would be right *ma chèr*, but hunters doan have dose kinds of resources."

An idea blinks to life, and I frown. Mary is right. There *should* be resources available to all hunters. I don't know if it's money or simply time they lack, but…

"Emma, are you listening?" Cass snaps his fingers, pulling my attention back to him.

"Sorry. What were you saying?"

"Woman, I be tryin' to save your life, and you're daydreamin'."

I start to unwrap Mary's sandwich, and Cass snatches it out of my hand. "Wha' did I just say?"

"Uh, not to be daydreaming?" I try to get the biscuit back, but he hands it off to Eric.

"You are experiencin' de curse's hunger. De more you eat, de hungrier you will become."

"And we don't want that?" Eric drawls, and I detect a little more New Orleans in his voice. Since we moved here last year, we've all started to take on notes of that accent. Hard to live somewhere and not.

"No, de more she gives in, de more de curse thickens in her blood, and de faster she dies."

"Dies?" Dan's hand instinctively wraps around mine. Not sure if it's to comfort him or me, but I'll take it either way. The conversation I had with Cass about the roogie before Silas showed up starts to emerge from my memories, and I need all the comfort I can get.

"A Rougarou is a beast born of a curse. He partially shifts into a beast, most typically dat of a wolf. He retains his human form, wit' a few variations. His hands and feet grow claw-like talons, and his face…" Cass shudders. Was he there when the thing killed his family?

"His face?" Dan prompts.

Cass takes a deep, fortifying breath. "His face more closely resembles dat of a wolf without de long snout. It's hideous."

"It is," I agree, remembering looking into its eyes when I was fighting with it.

"During de day, he looks like he always does, a regular man or woman. It's only at night, when de moon rules de sky, dat de beast emerges, and his hunger overrules everything in him dat is human. He attacks and kills just to ease de hunger."

"How is this different from a werewolf?" Mary asks.

"Dere is a werewolf, and a shifter in de supernatural or preternatural world, as some call it. De werewolf is born from catching an infection of de blood, lycanthropy. When the moon changes, the wolf takes over and dere is no'tin left of de person dey were, only de wolf. He hunts wit'out t'ought."

"Like your monster movie werewolves, then?" Eric slides down the wall until his butt hits the floor and inhales more of his coffee.

"*Oui*, for lack of a better analogy." Cass nods. "Den you have shifters. Magic created dem back during de dawn of time. Dey be born shifters, be it wolves, cats, birds, and other creatures. Dey retain dere human mind and animal instincts while in animal form. Dese are fierce adversaries when we have to hunt dem, and not to be underestimated."

"So, shifters are dangerous and on the list of things to hunt. Got it."

"No' necessarily. Shifters are not evil creatures. Dey just go a bit furry. Some of dem, well, dey can go bad just like humans. When dat happens, the shifter community usually puts down dere own, but sometimes, we get called in to help."

"They're not on the hunter's hit list, then?"

"No' usually," Cass says, twisting his hands. "Den we get to de Rougarou."

He's slipped back into his easy accent, so I have to wonder if he's accepted me and Dan and all the people in this room. He's usually not so open around them all. It gives me hope I may not have lost a good friend.

"De Rougarou is a beast born of a curse, usually voodoo, but no' always. It's a man or woman who has been cursed to kill for one full moon cycle, thirty days, usually. The sickness eats away at their humanity until nothing remains of de person in de end. The curse drives dem mad until the last day of de moon cycle. Dey die in de end. It is a cruel way to go."

"How does this transfer to me and you?"

"We got bit. The curse, like lycanthropy, is carried in de blood and transferred to anyone who is bitten and survives. We begin to show signs of de sickness, and unless we kill de beast dat did dis to us, we will die de same death at de end of de moon cycle. By killing it, we effectively break de curse, and we woan end up like the Rougarou."

"So, we have a full moon cycle to find and kill it?" That's a month. Surely, we can track it in that length of time.

The grimace tells me that is not the case.

"I had Robert check around. Dere have been cases reported of missing people since de beginning of de month, Emma. It's now five days from Halloween. De full moon ends on November third. We have eight days."

"Eight days?" I whisper. I'm not sure I'll be able to move anytime soon. Eight days is a death sentence.

"*Oui*." He looks down at his leg. He's not going to be moving any sooner than I will.

"What are we gonna do?"

He looks hesitant, and I know I'm not gonna like what he has to say.

"I was t'inkin' last night about wha' you said, wha' you are."

Mary and Eric both look up, their expressions guarded.

"When we were out in de swamp, you seemed to gain strength when you were falling down, almost passing out. Was dat because of your demon side you could do dat?"

I nod.

"If you let dat part of yourself out, could you ignore your wounds and hunt?"

"Theoretically, yes. When my demon blood activates, it ignores the wounds of my body. All of this," I wave at the injuries, "is like a paper cut."

"You went toe to toe with de Rougarou and walked away alive because of de demon part of you. No one has faced one and lived before."

"You did," Eric points out.

Cass shakes his head. "*Non*, it tossed me aside and went after Emma. It sensed de biggest threat was from her."

"You said 'we' have to kill it to escape the curse." I hold onto Dan's hand with a death grip. The thought of giving myself over to all the darkness inside of me scares me more than almost anything. "Does that mean if I kill it and you aren't a part of the killing blow, then you still die?"

"*Oui, chèr*, dat is exactly wha' it means."

"But why?" Mary asks. "What does it matter?"

"Is all a part of de curse. The why is in de casting of it."

"How does the curse go?" If we can figure out what exactly is in the casting of it, as he says, then maybe we can stop it without having to kill the thing ourselves, and I won't have to go dark side.

"I doan know, *chèr*. Only de person who cast it would know dat."

"What about that voodoo lady in the swamp? Would she know?"

He shrugs. "She might have been de one to do it."

"Can the thing hurt her if she's the one who did cast the curse?"

"If it were me, I'd build an exempt clause into that particular curse." Eric stretches his legs out in front of him and yawns. Freaking yawns when we're being told I could die from this curse.

"What?" he asks when I give him the stink eye.

"Are we boring you?" I snark, my biggest weapon against my own fear.

"Don't be like that," Eric says. "Me and Mary slept all night in the waiting room. I'm just tired, Hathaway. You know I love you, girl, and I'll do whatever I have to do to keep you safe."

And now I feel bad. I know Eric loves me. He's not only my best friend, but he's taken the place of a big brother in my life. He's family, and I need to keep my snarkiness in check.

"Sorry."

He tilts his head in acknowledgement. I don't say I'm sorry often.

"Back to the question. Is the voodoo lady exempt?"

"I'm no' sure," Cass says. "She was heavily warded against it, so she ei'der didn't cast it, or she's not safe from it."

"Well, this is a job for Ezekiel Crane."

Dan stops me before I can even pick up the phone. "What are you doing?"

"Calling my dad to get answers from the voodoo lady."

His lip curls. He knows my father is not exactly above using criminal methods to get what he wants. It goes against everything Dan is as a police officer. I understand that, but I don't have time for his morals to get in the way. We have eight days to fix this.

"You know how he's going to get those answers." The not-so-gentle reproach is telling. Dan may accept the fact that Zeke's my dad, but the cop in him can't accept him.

"Dan. You don't know what I saw last night. She tried to get my blood. You have my blood, you have power over me. She's not someone you can just go question. She's dangerous, and it requires someone just as dangerous to deal with her."

"He might hurt her."

"He might," I agree, "but in this case, it's her or me, and I choose me."

That doesn't sit well with Officer Dan, but he doesn't try to stop me again when I call Zeke and explain the situation to him. He promises to get the answers we need by the end of the day. I push down every ounce of remorse I have. She doesn't deserve it.

"Mattie…"

"Don't Mattie me." I cut him off. "That woman was going to let me bleed to death last night because she knew I was part demon. Wasn't going to offer any help until she found out who my father was."

"What do you mean, she was going to let you bleed to death?" Dan's eyes crinkle with something very close to rage.

"She be telling you de truth." Cass's fingers twist in the hospital gown he's wearing. "She knew what Emma was de moment she saw her and refused to help her. She wasn't even gonna call de ambulance for me until Emma made her. Doan pity de voodoo priestess. She doan need or deserve it."

His fist clenches, and the hand holding mine spasms. The sword on his back flares so brightly it hurts the eyes. "See, I'm not the only one who gets mad and goes a little loopy when our lives are threatened."

"I think it's sweet." Mary smiles.

Cass pushes back from the bed the tiniest bit. I'm not sure what he can see, but he senses the shift in Dan's mood.

The nurse comes in before anyone can respond and shoos them out while she does her hourly vitals check. The doctor arrives on her heels and announces I need another CT scan. He won't say why, only that he wants to do a repeat one. I think maybe my brain is trying to crack again. My demon half, combined with my reaping abilities I'm not supposed to have to begin with, might be a little too much.

I hope that's not the case, but I have a feeling.

A very bad feeling.

The next person to walk into my hospital room isn't the person I'm expecting. It's the one person I want to see almost more than Dan.

Nancy Moriarity.

My old social worker from North Carolina moved to New Orleans a few months ago, and she and my father have been dating, something they hid from me for a bit because they were unsure of my reaction.

How did I feel about that?

Fan-freaking-tastic!

I love Nancy. She's been my number one supporter since she came to collect me at the police station that first day. I'd run away from social services in New Jersey and gotten myself to North Carolina. I'd been caught stealing from one of the local grocery stores and arrested. Nancy took one look at me and decided I was worth the effort.

It's because of her I turned my life around, stopped being so bratty, and worked to get my grades up so I could get a scholarship. She taught me the value of having someone at your back, someone always on your team.

She may not be my mother, but she feels like it.

And I've missed her.

"Hey." She smiles softly as she approaches the bed. "Your dad said it was okay for me to come and check on you. You okay? You look a little rough."

"I look like dog meat."

"Well, you do, but I wasn't going to say it." Her brown eyes light up with laughter, and it always shocks me how dark they are in comparison to the almost milky cream color of her skin. Had she not told me that her mother was black and her father white, I don't know if I'd have known. I might have suspected Hispanic, but I guess it doesn't matter. She's a beautiful person inside and out, and that's what counts the most.

"Eric already has, so you might as well too."

"That boy." She shakes her head and sits in the chair beside the bed. "He's a charmer when he's not being a brat."

Nancy fell in love with Eric. I think it's the social worker in her that recognized a lost little boy. Eric had been a ghost whose soul I reaped. When Jake died, his soul moved on, but his body remained. I transferred Eric's soul into Jake's empty shell of a body. It gave Mr. and Mrs. Owens back their son, albeit a son who had no memories of being that boy, and it gave Eric a chance at having a real family who would love him no matter what. He'd been a foster kid in real life, and the chance at happily-ever-after was always the goal.

"Where's Dan?" Nancy pulls my attention back to her.

"He went to find me food. The hospital

stuff is nasty." Not that I didn't eat it when it came. I'm starving. I am trying not to stuff myself so I don't go mad, but it's hard. The smell of food is enough to make me cry right now.

"That man loves you."

It doesn't escape my notice that she called Eric a boy and Dan a man, even though, technically, Eric is older, having died at the age of eighteen in 1994. Not that she knows that, of course. Nancy's in the dark about the supernatural world. Zeke is going to have to 'fess up if he wants things to go past casual with her.

"I know." For the first time since the swamp, a real smile creeps across my face. He does that for me. Even in my darkest nightmares, he's there to protect me. Sometimes even from myself.

"Ezekiel tells me he's moving down here after his mother's trial."

I nod, still smiling. It's selfish of me to want him here, away from both his birth and adoptive families, but I can't help it. I'm a selfish person, never said I wasn't, but I try not to be with Dan. When it comes to him being there or here, there's no choice. I want him here. Even if we weren't together, I'd still want him here. I need him.

I notice Nancy shiver. I know for a fact I have the heat on. While it doesn't actually get cold often in the south, I keep the heat on because I'm *always* cold. Too much ghost energy. Nancy should be sweating, not freezing. I take a deep breath and close my eyes. Does it feel colder in here to me? Maybe, but I'm not sure. Maybe something slid in while I wasn't looking? Ghosts can hide from me when they want. Not for long, but it doesn't take long for them to get up to no good either.

"Emma?"

It's strange to hear her call me that. But unlike Dan, she understands my need to leave everything bad that happened to me in the past, and that includes the name Mattie Louise Hathaway.

"Yeah?"

"Where did you go just now?"

"Just thinking about Dan." My eyes hunt the room, looking at every shadow. *Please don't show up while Nancy is here*. It would be my luck for a ghost to decide now is the perfect time to badger me about helping them.

"You have a keeper there."

"He said he's going to marry me when I'm ready."

Nancy's smile widens. "That man."

A cold so sharp it's downright painful settles beside me, and I don't want to turn my head. I know something awful will be waiting.

Ignore it, and it'll go away. Ignore it, and it'll go away.

It's been my mantra since I was five.

"So, what's going on with you and Zeke?"

Her eyes dim a little. "I don't know."

"What do you mean?"

"He's been a little distant recently." I don't think she meant to tell me that. She looks too startled. People can't lie to me, though. They tell me the truth whether they want to or not, a gift I inherited from Zeke.

"He's had a lot on his mind lately," I tell her. "There've been some problems with his food shipments to Africa, and I know it's getting to him. He can't just take the supplies back from villages that need them as much as their destination."

Her expression softens. Not many people know about all the good things Ezekiel Crane does. He keeps it that way. He likes people to fear him. They'll be less likely to cross him.

"He was telling me about that. I know it bothers him that he can't help them all."

"Once he gets it sorted, I think it'll free up some of that worry."

Cold, dead fingers run up and down my arm. I barely stop the shudder. Nope, not looking.

"I hope so."

"He really likes you, Nancy." I reach over to grasp her hand, partly to comfort her and partly to get away from the ghost trying to get my attention. "Don't worry."

"He thinks I'll run when I find out who he is."

Her gasp is a sure sign she didn't mean to let that little tidbit of information loose.

"He's got a reputation, Nancy. My dad

has done some very bad things and probably will again, but that doesn't mean he's a bad man."

"No, it doesn't." She squeezes my fingers. "I see all the good he does and how he is with you. Even how he is with his mother. That woman bosses him as much as I do."

I laugh. "Yeah, Gram is a bit of a terror. I think she's one of the few people Zeke's afraid of."

"She scares me a little too," Nancy admits with a giggle, and I join her. The thought of anyone scaring Nancy is too ridiculous to contemplate. I've seen her go toe-to-toe with some downright vicious people and come out the other side without a scratch on her.

"Don't get mired down in aspects of his life that have nothing to do with how he feels about you, okay?" I bring it back to a serious tone. I don't want Zeke to lose her because he is having issues telling her the truth. "Zeke cares, and that's what's important."

"People have been telling me things, things that are quite disturbing."

"People are gonna talk, Nancy, and Zeke is someone who does very bad things, but that part of his life has nothing to do with you or me. Focus on who he is when he's with you."

"You think I should ignore what everyone's telling me? You're not helping, here, Emma."

"I'm not gonna tell you he doesn't partake in criminal activities. Heck, you've seen my rap sheet. He and I are the same. We do what we need to do to protect ourselves and the people we love. We won't apologize for that. Doesn't mean we're bad people."

"Of course not." Nancy jumps up and hugs me. I wince when her hand grazes my shoulder. "You are a wonderful young lady, and I am so proud of you."

"Thanks." I one-arm hug her back. My left arm is pretty useless with an IV needle stuck in it. "I love you, Nancy."

She goes completely still at those words, words I should have told her a long time ago.

"I know I didn't tell you before, but I do. You saved me from myself all those years ago, and you never stopped fighting for me even when I deserved it. Without you, God only knows where I would be today. So, thank you for that."

"Oh, sweetheart." Tears shimmer in her eyes. "I love you too."

"Zeke's a guy, so he's an idiot. Just don't listen to the rumors and focus on the man himself, okay? I don't want to lose you because he's being stupid."

She chuckles softly and hugs me tighter. "No matter what happens with your father and me, you will never lose me. That, I can promise."

I hope that's true, but in my experience, it's not always the case. Nancy has been with me for years, though, so maybe she'll stick around.

"I brought you something." She leans down and snatches up her purse. Her very large purse. Brenda from *The Closer* black purse large. She pulls out a brand-new sketch pad and some charcoal pencils. "I thought you might want these, as I'm not sure when they're letting you out."

"Hopefully tomorrow. No more

headaches, and I've had my twenty-four hours of antibiotics. I think I'm only still here because Zeke's pitching a fit."

"That sounds about like him, but you have to remember, he almost lost you once after having just found you. He's scared."

"I know. It's why I'm *not* pitching a fit even though I hate hospitals."

"You're a good girl."

"Shh," I say, horrified. "I have a rep to protect."

Nancy bursts out laughing. "I have to go, sweetheart. I just wanted to check on you while I was here. I need to go back downstairs. I got called in on a case."

"I hope everything isn't as bad as it can be."

"Me too." She sighs. "I won't know until the doctor can speak with me. You get some rest and listen to the doctors."

"Promise. Besides, I have some new toys to keep me busy." I nod down to the art supplies on my lap.

When Nancy leaves, the smile slips from my face. The ghost is still there, standing right by my bed. Do I look? Or

APRYL BAKER

just ignore it?

The icy cold creeps closer, and I know ignoring this one is going to be impossible. Taking a fortifying breath, I turn my head.

And scream.

It isn't a ghost standing by my bed.

It's a shade.

Creatures from The Between, the place that separates this plane of existence from the next one. It devours souls. Sometimes they get out and go looking for anything they can find to ease their hunger. Food in The Between is hard to come by, thanks to the reapers who usually ferry souls from this place to the next.

And as much ghost energy as I have, I'm probably the best meal it'll find this side of the Mississippi.

There's nothing to defend myself with. I can't open up a circle of The Between.

I've been afraid to since I consumed all those wraiths. The darkness in me begs to do it, to swallow it whole, and I refuse to give in. I don't have iron or salt to ward it off either.

All I have is the sketchpad in my hand, and that's not going to save me.

The thing is made up of wispy black strands of shadows that resemble a shredded cloak. This is what everyone thinks a reaper is. Someone at some point in time must have seen one, and the images sprang from there.

The glowing red eyes from deep within its hooded cowl study me.

Why hasn't it attacked yet?

It reaches out a hand, and I flinch away from it. I don't want that thing touching me. A hiss escapes where its mouth should be. Grasping the edge of the bed, I yank myself away from it and stand. Pain slices through my entire body. The cuts are deep and swollen, more painful today than they were when first inflicted. It doesn't help that I refused pain meds either.

The shade floats through the bed,

intent on...heck if I know, but I'm not staying around to find out. Jerking the IV out of my arm, I stumble toward the door. I doubt it will follow me out, but then again, it decided to show up while Nancy was here.

The IV alarm is shouting at me, and I fumble with the doorknob. Why did Nancy close it when she left?

I don't make it. It floats right up against me, freezing me in place. Its stagnant breath blows against my cheek, winter to my fall. Its hands come to rest against the door on either side, effectively trapping me. Leaning in, it sniffs all along my face, and I shudder from the horrible feeling.

The door shoves at my back, but I'm afraid to move.

"Miss Crane!" the nurse shouts.

The thing hisses again, the sound almost frustrated.

The door shoves again, and I'm pushed forward into the creature, and I fall, landing on my hands and knees. I went right through it, and bile rises in my throat. Coughing, I try to fight the urge to hurl, but when its hands grip my shoulder, I can't. Hot liquid spews out of my mouth and onto the floor. Shudders wrack me as its claw-like fingers dig into the wound on my shoulder. Intense pain sickens me all over again, and I'm vomiting. It just won't stop.

I try to crawl away from it, but it's stuck. Weak and with my vision a little blurry, I reach out for anyone to help me. The nurse is there, but she can't see this thing attached to me, feeding off me.

One person comes to mind, one person who can see this thing and help me, and I shout his name, not caring if the nurse thinks I'm crazy. I need Kane.

He appears a few feet away, looking irritated until he sees what's happening. Anger replaces his irritation and he stalks forward, his own reaping skills out in full force. The thing attached to me flinches, and its hands loosen enough for me to jerk free from its grasp. I don't even care that I land in my own vomit. It's better than the horror of being fed upon by something that dark.

The nurse calls for help, but I keep my

eyes on Kane. He lashes out, and the thing is caught in his web of power. Thick cords of white, smoky ropes have latched onto the thing, and he's drawing it to him and away from me. He nods once and mouths he'll be back when he and the thing disappear into an open doorway to The Between.

And that's when my body decides I've had enough and gives out. For once, I don't even try to fight the dark. I'm too exhausted.

***

The lights are low the next time I wake up. Dan is on his phone talking quietly, but not so low I can't hear him. It's his mom. He's arguing about being here with me instead of in Charlotte. Her trial starts on November first, less than two weeks from now. He promised to be there for her. I hate that he feels like he has to pick and choose. Moms are important, even moms who don't particularly like me.

I reach out and nudge his hand.

Worried brown eyes snap to me, and he tells his mom he's gonna have to call her back. In that moment, all his focus zeroes in on me, and I am the complete center of his world. I've read about that feeling in books before, about how intense the emotion is when you realize you're so loved that nothing and no one else matters, that you're it. The books don't do that feeling justice.

Unwanted tears spring to my eyes. I was never a crier before Dan Richards, but he thawed the ice around my heart, and I feel so much more now because of him.

"Hey, now, what's this?" Dan takes my face in his hands, and his eyes search mine, worried. "Are you in pain? Do I need to get the nurse?"

"No." I drag in a tear-choked breath. "I…"

"What is it, baby?"

And there the tears go. He went and made me feel like I am the only person in the world who means anything to him. Jumping up, Dan wraps me in his arms and holds me as tight as he can without hurting me. He has no idea why I'm crying, and honestly, neither do I. I'm emotional. More so than normal. Every little thing is a thousand times more sensitive. I feel it all, and it hurts, even the love and joy his touch brings. It's too much, but there isn't a force in this world that can make me move.

"I love you," I whisper. I don't tell him enough. I say "I love you" to him all the time, but never like this, never with the force of everything in me behind it. He goes still, realizing how deep my confession goes. Dan knows me better than anyone, and he understands how hard saying those words is, and that I really mean them past a simple declaration of love and affection. I love him to the very core of my being with everything I have.

"I love you too." His lips graze my temple. "What's wrong?"

"I…" Taking a deep breath, I try to calm down, but my emotions are all over the place. "Everything is wrong."

"Tell me." He gently pushes me over so he can climb in bed with me. I fall against his chest and let the steady beating of his heart soothe me. Dan is safe, he's warm, and he's home. I once thought of Eli as home, but that was just a shade of what I feel when Dan holds me. I had so many walls up because Dan hurt me once, so much that I blocked what I felt for him. I convinced myself what we had was just friendship, but it is so much more than that.

When he kissed me for the first time, I understood how wrong I'd been. All those walls crumbled in the face of that one kiss, and I understood the true meaning of home. It's where you're wanted, where you're safe, and where you're loved. Dan is that for me. Right here, curled up against him, is my home.

"I want to go get out of here."

"That's not a good idea, Squirt. The nurse said she found you throwing up, and then you passed out."

My nose curls. I remember that. I fell in my own puke. "Do I stink?"

When he doesn't say anything, I know I do. So not staying here smelling like puke. I try to move away, but his arms tighten. "No, you don't. I love you, stink and all."

This man. Nancy's words echo in my head. He's willing to put up with my stinky-ness, all because I'm upset. I don't deserve him. He's everything that is good in this world, and I'm...well, I'm my father's daughter.

"I'm not safe here. I want to leave."

His sigh is telling. "Mattie, you're not well enough if you were throwing up."

"I was throwing up because a shade slipped in the room and attacked me."

"What?" He stares down at me.

"Didn't you feel how weak I got, how I couldn't move?"

He nods. "I assumed it was because you got sick."

"No. It was a shade. I can't put up salt barriers or have iron weapons here to defend myself. I couldn't fight it off. I want to go somewhere safe, Dan. Please."

"Your dad…"

"Will fight me tooth and nail on this, and you know it, so don't even think about calling him." I shoot a glare up at him. "Take me home."

His lips purse. "I don't think…"

"What happens if another one comes and I'm alone again? With nothing and no one to protect me? What then, Officer Dan?"

And I know I have him. Dan's main focus is always to protect me. He can't argue that point. I'm not safe here. He can't be here all the time. I need to be somewhere the bad things can't get to me.

"Let me talk to the doctor and see what your CT scans said."

I grin in triumph, and even the scorching glare he sends me isn't enough to wipe the grin off my face. The doctor was in this morning while he went to get coffee downstairs and told me my scans were okay. Not good, but okay. There were signs of seizure activity, but nothing severe. He wanted me to see a neurologist immediately. I will do that, but not until we figure out this roogie situation.

It takes about an hour to talk to the doctor, sign everything, and get out of there. I know it's against medical advice, but honestly, I need to be out of there so we can start working on the roogie situation. And I want to feel safe to go to sleep tonight. I can't do that wondering if a ghost or another shade is going to be paying me a visit.

Dan stops at the local Walmart to find me some pajamas. I'm still wearing the hospital gown, since my clothes were destroyed. He cuts the engine of the rental car and turns to me. Obviously, I can't go in and shop for myself, but he doesn't want to leave me in the car either.

"I got this." I do a mental shout for Kane. I want to speak with him, anyway. It only takes a minute for him to pop into the back seat. Dan jumps when he appears. "See? I have a built-in babysitter."

"Hey! I might have been busy."

"Were you?"

"No."

"See?" I smile at them both.

Dan is uneasy around Kane because he was the reaper who came for Dan when he almost died. I fought him off long enough for Silas to hide Dan until we could figure out how to keep him alive. Dan was supposed to die that day. It was written in the grand scheme of things for him to die. He's not supposed to be here, and it's unnatural. The powers that be worry because he chose me over anyone whose death resulted in him not moving on. Meg being one of them. But like I told Dan, had she not died that night, she would have died at the hands of a psycho who would have tortured her. He saved her from that fate.

Do I believe that? I choose to because it makes me feel better. Dan and I will always choose each other, and that scares everyone upstairs. Dan is the most unselfish person I know, but when it came to that decision, to stay or go, he chose the selfish option. He chose me.

"You need a babysitter?" Kane asks and leans back. He's wearing jeans and a dark green t-shirt, his standard attire. I still don't know if reapers were once humans who took on that role after death, or if they're Angels or some other being. I really need to ask him about that eventually. I know I'm a living reaper, so humans *can* become reapers, but did they start out as something else? Questions for another time, though.

I can't go in there in nothing but a hospital gown. Heck, I don't even have on underwear, something Dan is very aware of when Kane leans forward and whistles. His eyes narrow, and he shifts closer.

"What you doing out in your skivvies, girl?"

Skivvies? See, this is one of those times when what comes out of his mouth is so much older than he looks. Just how old is he?

"What's a skivvy?"

He rolls his eyes, very much the twenty-ish-something he looks. "Why you out with nothing on underneath that thing?"

"I jumped bail with Dan's help."

Kane frowns. "They didn't release you?"

"I wasn't safe there."

His frown remains, but he nods. "I don't know where that thing came from. I swept the hospital earlier today to make sure you were safe. Even warned away most of the ghosts."

"You did?"

"Yeah, I think you have enough to worry about without getting bombarded by souls too stubborn to move on. Some of the ones downstairs you really want to stay away from."

The morgue. Been there, done that, won't do it again.

My phone beeps before I can say anything. I put it on charge the minute we got into the car. It's lit up with dozens of missed messages all from one person— my brother, Aleric Nathaniel Buchard. I don't think he knows what happened. He and I have settled into a routine of texting at least once a day. When I didn't answer, he probably got worried.

Kane leans forward, his forearm resting on the back of my seat, brushing against my hair. Dan lets out a sound I've never heard from him before, and it's enough to move Kane back.

"I'm not after your girl."

"Don't touch her."

Wow.

"Dan…" He cuts me off with a look. He's downright territorial.

"*Capiche?*"

Kane nods.

"I am gonna go in and find you some clothes. And underwear." The last part is said on a little bit of a snarl with a look directed at Kane. "Lock the doors until I get back."

"Dan?" I stop him before he can shut the door.

"Yeah, Squirt?"

"Will you get me something to eat?"

He looks ready to disagree. He was there for the whole hunger conversation this morning. Eating will make me go mad faster.

"I threw up all my food. There's nothing in there, and if I don't eat, I might pass out again."

His worry for me wars with his need to protect me. "Okay. Just something small, though."

"Anything to take away this gnawing feeling in my gut."

He leans in and kisses my nose. "Stay safe."

When he's shut the door and waited for me to hit the locks, I turn to Kane. "I have a problem."

"I figured."

"Ever since I took in all those wraiths, the darkness in me is growing. I'm having seizures again."

"Your seizures were due to your reaping abilities…"

"No, it was a combination of everything, not just my reaping abilities. I got Rhea to lock everything but that away. None of those abilities went away, but the headaches did. Now that my demon side is awake and growing, the headaches are back. My seizures are back."

"That's not good, Emma."

"No, it's not."

"Do you think you can get Rhea to shut them down again?"

"Probably, but that's not the biggest problem."

"Dying isn't your biggest problem?" He gives me a cray-cray look.

"No. I keep having the urge to do bad things, to do horrible, awful things."

116

"The demon half of you," he surmises.

"I think that's only made it worse. This feeling has been there since I took in all those wraiths, Kane. You told me it was a bad thing, and I didn't listen. I'm listening now. How do I get rid of this?"

Kane reaches out a hand and places it against my forehead. He closes his eyes, and I feel his own abilities sink into me, searching. When he pulls back, he looks as worried as I feel.

"It's taken root around your soul. It's weird. It's like it's filling in cracks where your soul is loose, like it was pulled out then put back, but all the glue hasn't hardened. That darkness has filled all those spots, and every crack and fissure you already had is full of the dark. This isn't good, Emma."

"What do we do?"

"I don't know. I need to talk to people who know more about this than I do."

"The people who want me dead?" I shake my head. "No. This could give them exactly what they've been looking for to put me down."

He knows I'm right. "Then what do

you want me to do?"

"Just dig around, see what you can find out, and I'll talk to Silas. You were right about my soul. Silas pulled it out to make a point about how fragile it was. That gave the wraiths and all their darkness the ability to set up house and nest."

"The easiest solution is probably talking to your mother."

I know that, but I don't want to. Talking to Rhea is the absolute last choice. She abandoned me to a woman who wanted to sacrifice my soul as a blood payment to a Fallen Angel. Granted, she didn't know that, but come on. You make a deal with a demon to create a child with certain abilities, you have to know no good will come of it.

Out of the three women who could claim the title "mother," only Claire Hathaway earned that right. She took care of me. Even trying to kill me when I was five was her way of protecting me. If I wasn't here, then the bad things couldn't come for me. Took me years to understand that, but I do now, and I love her more fiercely than anyone else. She died that day, but she still protects me. She was the one to save me after I shattered my soul to save my sister and every innocent child in the world from Deleriel.

"I'm assuming you don't want the boyfriend to know about this?"

I ignore the censure in his voice. "I'll tell him eventually, but he's worried enough about me as it is. We just need to get done with this roogie thingy first."

"Roogie?" Kane cocks his head. "What's a roogie?"

"I can't remember the name. It's like a werewolf, but not really."

"A shifter?"

"No, the other one."

"A Rougarou?"

"Yup, that's it."

"Did it do all that damage to you?"

"Yeah. One attacked me and Cass in the swamp the other night, and now we're both infected."

"You both have to kill it, then."

"That's what Cass says. We just have to figure out who it is. Zeke is questioning the voodoo lady." Speaking of…

I pick up my phone and shoot him a quick text to let him know I checked out of the hospital because of random shades attacking and then cut off my phone. I'm not up for a lecture, and I don't want him tracking my phone either. I just want one night of peace and quiet.

"How long you have?"

"About eight days."

He lets out a whistle. "You're in it deep, Crane."

Dan knocks on the window, and I unlock the doors. He's got his phone to his ear, and he looks alarmed. Got to be Zeke.

"Zeke?" I mouth the word, and he nods. I hold my hand out for the phone, and he gives it over with no argument. Coward. "Papa, we're fine. I just needed out of there. The doctor said I was good to go. I need to be somewhere safe and where I can get one good night of rest."

Zeke lets out a long string of colorful phrases in both French and English. "Fine. How far are you from the house?"

"I'm not coming to the house tonight.

I'm going somewhere quiet. I'll be by the house in the morning."

"What do you mean, you're not coming to the house? Are you going back to your dorm room?"

"No."

Five.

Four.

Three.

"You are not spending the night alone with…"

"Goodnight, Papa." I hang up on him and turn the phone off before handing it back to Dan.

"Why did you cut it off?"

"Do you want him to track your phone?"

His face pales.

I laugh out loud at his expression.

"And on that note, I'm out. I'll dig around and find you when I have some information, yeah?"

"Thanks, Kane."

"No worries, little one." He poofs very much like Silas does. It's unnerving on the best of days, and even more so when I'm freaked out.

"Here." Dan shoves one of the bags at me. "I got you the warmest pajamas I could find. Louisiana doesn't believe in flannel in the winter."

"Doesn't get cold enough." I take the bag and dig through it. Dan indeed got me a bra and undies. Not sure the bra is gonna fit. Never leave it up to a man to guess a woman's bra size. His face flames when he sees what I'm holding. I would have given anything to see him walking around in the bra section. His face must have been cherry red the whole time. "Did the cashier ask you about these?" I hold up the bra and matching underwear set. "I bet she thought you were a crossdresser."

His eyes widen, and he busts out laughing. "I think she could tell those wouldn't fit me. They're too small."

He's got me there. "Turn around."

His eyebrows tilt upward.

I raise the underwear, and his face doesn't flame this time. His eyes heat with a whole new kind of emotion. It stirs butterflies to life in my stomach, and my own blood simmers at that look.

"Dan?"

He blinks and gets out of the car. He could have just turned around, but then I remember that look. Maybe he did need to get out of the car. I pull the tags off the underwear and slip them on quickly. The bra is a little too snug, and I feel like I'm gonna pop out of it, but it'll do for now. Digging around in the bag, I find a pair of gray bottoms with a long-sleeved black t-shirt that probably isn't a pajama top. He didn't go for girly. He went for warmth. They aren't exactly thick, but at least they cover me. I knock on the door when I'm dressed, and he slips back in. His eyes sweep over me, the heat in them still blazing.

"Warmer?"

"Yeah." We both know I'm not talking about the pajamas, but then neither is he, really.

"You want to go back to your dorm? I'm guessing you're hiding from your father."

"No, I don't want to go back to the dorm and listen to Mary and Eric badger me about checking out of the hospital."

"Then you *do* want to go back to your dad's?"

"No."

Five.

Four.

Three.

His eyes narrow, and that heat blazes to new heights.

"Where do you want to go, Mattie?"

"Somewhere quiet and safe. With you. Just you."

He stares at me for a long time before he starts the car and pulls out of the Walmart parking lot.

We settle on The Country Inn and Suites. It isn't fancy like Zeke would have gotten, but it is clean, and it's all we need. Thanks to a convention in town, all we could get was a room with a king size bed. The couch does have a pullout. That's the first thing Dan checks for. It's sweet. He never pushes me, and I can feel how much he wants to push. The heat in his eyes when he looks at me is a testament to that, but he puts my needs above his own. He loves me like that.

"This okay?" He gestures to the room. "I know it's not what you're used to…"

I put a finger against his lips. "I shop at

Walmart and get hives whenever I look at the debit card Zeke makes me carry. This is more than okay."

His smile is a little nervous. Not that I blame him. I'm nervous too.

"You still hungry?"

"Starved."

He goes over to the Walmart bag and pulls out a box of Hot Pockets. "I figured this would be better than ordering pizza."

My stomach grumbles, and I snort. "I'd rather have the pizza."

He laughs and pulls out a roll of paper towels, then tosses the plastic bag to me. While he's busy with the microwave, I sort through the bag. He bought bandages, medical tape, and antibacterial cream. He remembered I need to change my bandages without me reminding him.

"Hey, I picked up your antibiotics at the pharmacy too. They're in one of the bags. What time are they due, do you know?"

"Uhhh...no clue?" I hadn't even thought about that.

"When was the last time they gave them to you?"

"IV, remember?"

He frowns and looks at his watch. "It's a little after nine now. I guess we'll just start them at midnight so it'll be easier to remember."

The scent of the Hot Pockets tickles my nose, and my stomach lets out a very loud grumble. Dan laughs and hands it over when the microwave dings. Then he puts in the other one. I don't think this is enough to eat, but I don't want to overeat either. Giving in to the hunger will cause me to succumb more quickly to the curse flowing in my blood.

"Uh, I should tell you something." He leans against the wall, looking down at his phone. He hasn't turned it on, but I can tell he's debating.

"What?"

"I called in backup."

"Backup?" I take a bite of the hot gooey goodness that is cheese and pepperoni. Oh, my gosh, it's so good. My stomach rumbles in agreement.

"I don't know anything about a Rougarou, so I called Caleb. He freaked out when I told him what happened, which in turn freaked me out even more. This is dangerous, Mattie. More so than I thought."

I know how dangerous it is. I'm the one feeling the effects of it—the hunger, the heightened emotions, the need to go prowling, looking for food.

"He's on his way down here."

"What?" I screech and almost drop my precious Hot Pocket. Almost.

He looks sheepish. "I called the one person I knew I could count on for help."

"Mary is not going to be happy."

"I'm more worried about you than Mary's feelings right now." The microwave dings, and he collects the second Hot Pocket before coming to sit on the bed next to me. "Here. Eat this before your gut crawls out and makes a meal out of us both."

"Not funny." Literally, it might do that at some point. I don't know. The hunger will take over and drive me.

Dan kisses my forehead then gets up to rummage through the Walmart bags. He pulls out a large container of salt and sets about salting the doors and windows.

Thank God he remembered that, but I'm no more surprised about that than him picking up my medication. He takes care of me. He always will.

Which is why I can't be mad at him calling Caleb.

I'm not eager to see Caleb any more than Mary is. He reminds me of Eli, and I don't want to remember that pain. It's always there, always a breath away from overpowering me. He sacrificed his life for me. It's a debt I can never repay.

"Why don't you go take a shower and get the ick off you? I think there's still some dried blood in your hair. I need to call Caleb and see when his flight gets in. We may need to go pick him up at the airport."

I nod and polish off the last of the Hot Pockets. My stomach protests when the food stops, but I ignore it. I can't afford to eat more. Picking up the bag with the bandages, I go into the bathroom and shut the door. Gingerly taking off the new clothes, I lay them on the back of the toilet then start the shower running.

It takes me a second to get up the

courage to look in the mirror. I know it's going to be bad, but holy cow, is it bad. I'm covered in bandages, some of them a little bloody. I probably broke a few of the wounds open when I tried to get away from the shade. Carefully, I start peeling them off and gasp at the damage. Good Lord, I thought the scars I had before were bad. These are definitely gonna trump those.

And some of the gashes have mangled the tattoos Silas put on me. Panic hits at the thought. These things protect me from so much. Thankfully, most of the damage is to the front of my body, but the tattoo that protects me from Angels wraps around my legs at certain points, and one gash cuts right through it. Silas is going to kill me.

My gaze lands on scars as familiar to me as the color of my eyes. Scars that have been there since I was five years old. Scars that will always be there to remind me of the day my mother attempted to kill me.

Back then, I had no idea why. I thought it was just a consequence of her drug addiction, that she'd done it because she was so high on heroin she had no idea what she was doing. As I got older, I knew better. She was high that day, but she knew what she was doing. I'd seen it in her eyes. Then when I finally learned the truth, that she did it to protect me, that she was the only woman who called herself "mother" who'd honestly done everything out of love for me, I couldn't hate her anymore.

Those scars reminded me of everything I was, who I am now, and who I hope to be one day. I can only strive to be as strong as my mama. She was and still is the bravest person I know.

Shaking my head, I remove the bandages, wincing when several stick to my skin. A shower is probably gonna hurt like nobody's business, but all this dirt left over from the attack can't help either. I'm sure the hospital cleaned me up as best they could, but there's just too much dried blood everywhere. Even in my hair, as Dan pointed out. I probably do stink to high heaven.

Stepping into the shower, I hiss when

the water blasts all my open wounds.

Maybe this wasn't such a good idea.

Pain and I don't get along.

I'm used to it, but I don't deliberately go looking for it either.

Clenching my teeth against the pain, I use the little bar of hotel soap to do a quick scrub of my body, careful of the wounds. My hair is a problem. I can't raise my arms. It's too painful. Settling for just rinsing out the worst of the mess, I finish quickly and get out, drying off and pulling my underwear back on.

After several failed attempts, I give up trying to rebandage some of the wounds. The one on my shoulder is the worst of the bunch. My arms are so sore and stiff, I can barely lift them. Putting my bra on had been almost impossible. If Mary were here, she'd help me. And she'd do it right too, her mom being a nurse and all.

Biting my lip, I weigh my options. I'm a mess, and no girl wants to see the heat in her boyfriend's eyes dim, but I can't leave these wounds untreated either. Antibiotics or not, infection is dangerous.

"Dan!"

There's a knock at the door seconds later. "You okay in there?"

"I need help." Sitting down on the towel I'd put in front of the tub, I pull the other one up over myself. Yeah, I'm still as shy as you can get when it comes to any kind of sexual situation. Probably because I'm still a virgin. I was never that girl who just gave it up. It's something special to me, and it deserves to go to the guy I love enough to spend the rest of my life with. Old fashioned, I know, but that's how I feel about it. I don't do casual sex or one-night stands. It was never my thing.

He opens the door so slowly, I can feel his hesitation. It would be funny if I weren't so embarrassed I want to crawl up under a rock and hide.

When his gaze lands on me sitting on the floor huddled under a towel, his lips tilt up. "Watcha doing down there, Squirt?"

"I can't raise my arms."

His expression softens. He kneels in front of me and without a word turns the faucet in the tub on then reaches up on the sink to grab the container for the ice. Gently, as if I'm made of glass, he leans my head over the tub and starts rinsing it out using the bin. He works in the shampoo a minute later, his fingers a caress. He doesn't say anything while he washes my hair, and I close my eyes, enjoying having my hair washed, and some of my embarrassment slips away.

When he's done, he grabs a dry towel and uses it to get most of the water out of my hair. "Better?"

"Do I still stink?"

"No." He wraps the towel around my head to keep my hair out of his way and sets about cleaning the wound on my shoulder. "I didn't know it took a chunk out of you."

"Yeah, trust me, watching it happen was way worse than seeing this."

"I'll bet." He uses the cotton balls to cover the wound in the cream before applying the large pad and wrapping it in gauze, careful of lifting my arm so he can wrap the shoulder. It's something Mrs. Cross would have done.

"Silas is going to pitch a fit." He

moves the towel so he can get to the wounds on my legs.

"I was thinking that too." My breath hitches at the feel of his fingers moving against the bare skin of my thigh. He goes still for a heartbeat at the sound, but then continues to patch up each wound, careful not to hurt me.

"Did you talk to Caleb?"

He nods. "He rented a car and is on his way over. I told him he could bunk on the pullout. There aren't many decent hotel rooms left. Some one- and two-star places, but we have room. If that's okay with you?"

"Yeah, I think it's a good idea." Having Caleb here will keep both our minds off the one subject I'm in no condition for.

"I thought so too. We need a buffer."

So, I'm not the only one thinking with my mind in the gutter.

"Did you get the ones on your stomach bandaged?"

I shake my head and almost groan out loud. It means pulling the towel down. All I'm wearing is my bra and panties.

He grips the towel and eases it away from me. I can't look him in the eye. I'm covered in bruises and jagged wounds. It's the least sexy thing you'll ever see.

"Mattie." His hushed word pulls my head up. He's not staring at me in disgust. Far from it. That heat is back in his eyes, but more than that, there is concern. "I don't think we should have left the hospital. These are bad."

"They look worse than they feel."

"Somehow, I doubt that." He reaches over and grabs the washcloth that had fallen into the tub and uses it to wash the edges of the wound. "This tear open when you fell?"

"I guess. I passed out, so I can't say for sure."

He makes a *tsk*-ing sound and continues to clean the deep wound and bandage it up. "The trouble you get into, woman."

"I was looking for a ghost, not a roogie," I point out in my own defense while trying to ignore the way his fingers burn against my skin. The feeling is that much more intense because of the curse eating away inside me.

He chuckles. "It's a Rougarou."

"Whatever."

"You're adorable, you know that?"

"I'm awesome."

"That you are." He reaches over and grabs the clothes I'd put on the toilet. "Now, let's get your awesome self into these before you freeze to death."

He stands and helps me up. It's only then I think he truly understands I'm standing here half naked in just a bra and panties. His entire body shifts closer even as he stares. I duck my head, all that embarrassment rushing back.

"Don't do that," he whispers.

"What?"

"Hide from me." He cups my face and pushes it up so I'm staring into fathomless brown eyes. "You're beautiful, Mattie Louise Hathaway, scars and all."

And my stomach does this funny little flip when his eyes fill up with more love than words can ever express. How can someone love me like this? The girl who got thrown away from foster home to foster home her entire life. I never knew what love was until Dan, never knew I was worth being loved, or that I could love someone in return.

He leans in and kisses me, the touch so soft, it's almost nonexistent, but I feel it just the same. "Come on, let's get you dressed before Caleb gets here. Wouldn't do to have him seeing my girl half naked."

A small smile tugs at my lips. I never get used to hearing him refer to me as his girl.

He helps me get dressed even though he doesn't have to. The shirt was difficult to get on and off before, and I wasn't looking forward to it again.

"Can I ask you something?"

"Sure." I follow him back out into the bedroom. It's a lot warmer than it was. One glance at the heating and cooling unit is enough to confirm the heat is on full blast.

He jumps on the bed and pats the place beside him. Gingerly, I climb up and settle into the mountain of pillows he'd piled up while I was in the bathroom. He had to have called down for extras. His arm snakes out and tugs me into his side. "The scars on your chest and stomach, the older ones, are those from your mother?"

I nod. Of course, he'd seen them.

He doesn't say anything, just hugs me to him. What is there to say to that, really? I'm sorry? Doesn't help.

"I don't blame her anymore."

"No?" His cheek comes to rest against my hair. "How did you forgive her?"

The uncertainty in his words speaks volumes about the real meaning of his questions. He's thinking about his mother and what she did. Ann Richards brutally killed his birth mother and stole him away from the Malones. She did it to protect him, and he's been trying to reconcile that since he found out. It can't be easy.

"My mother was protecting me the only way she knew how. Granted, had she not been a junkie, that might not have seemed like a reasonable solution, but I understand why she did."

"But how?" His tone is so pained, I

curl into him, offering the only comfort I can give. "How can you forgive something like that?"

"Because she loved me the same way your mom loves you." I look up at him. "Your mom did a horrible thing. I'm not excusing that or saying it's right. But she loves you. She raised you to be a good, honest man. Remember the hugs, the kisses, the times she sat with you when you needed her. Remember all that instead of everything else."

"It's hard. So hard when I look at Caleb and James and see what could have been. She took Amelia away from them, took me away from my family. It's eating me up inside trying to..." He breaks off and can't speak. Tears glitter in his eyes.

"I don't know what to say, Dan. All I can do is support you and be here for you the same way you always are for me. You love her, and she loves you, and I think in the end that's what counts the most, but it's up to you. I know you. You're a cop for a reason. Doing the right thing is important to you. Only you can decide what that is here. I won't judge you no matter what you decide."

"I love you, Squirt."

"I love you too, Officer Dan."

We sit like that for the longest time. I wish I could take away his pain, but I can't. Nothing I can say will make this war inside him better.

Only Dan can work through his feelings and settle on what he can live with.

But I'll be here for him when he does.

Caleb Malone.

Tall, dark, and handsome.

It's so obvious he and Dan are brothers. They look alike, with the same brown hair and eyes. Same cheekbones, same lips. When I first met Caleb, I couldn't help but think he reminded me of someone. He made me feel safe. It was because he was Dan's brother. Dan always makes me feel safe, and I guess his resemblance to Caleb caused the same feeling with his brother.

He also has that same "need to do the right thing" mindset Dan does.

Me? Not so much. I'll do what I have

to, no matter the consequences. I'm a professional liar and can usually get myself out of trouble, but not always. My rap sheet in Charlotte will speak to that.

"Mattie." Caleb smiles and opens his arms for a hug when he walks into the room. Seeing him is like a knife to the heart, but I push that down and hug him.

"Careful," Dan warns. "She's pretty cut up."

"You do get into trouble, don't you?" Caleb ruffles my hair when he lets me go. "How do you survive without us?"

"Please, you both know your life is downright boring without me."

Caleb laughs. "Don't ever change, Mattie."

"Never gonna." I go over and attempt to get back on the bed, but it's not so easy. My body feels like a massive bruise, and moving wasn't such a good idea.

Dan makes a sound, and then his arms are there, lifting me and setting me on the bed. "Ask for help."

"I'm not helpless," I grouch.

"I know, but I like helping you." He

smiles, and it sets off that odd feeling in my stomach. My cheeks flame at the look on his face. He leans in to kiss me.

Caleb clears his throat. "Brother in the room. I don't need my eyes scrubbed tonight."

Dan laughs and kisses my nose instead. "Thanks for coming, man."

"You call, I come." Caleb falls down on the couch. "This my bed?"

"It pulls out into a bed." Dan pulls the blankets down and helps me get under them.

"I made a few calls before I left. There's a woman down on Bourbon Street we need to go see tomorrow. She's a voodoo priestess and might be able to help us figure out who the Rougarou is."

"How?"

"Well, each spell a person casts leaves behind a magical fingerprint. We're hoping she can pick up that trail."

"How?"

"She'll need your blood."

"No." The word is out before he's even finished talking. "Absolutely not. I will not give my blood to someone who could use it against me."

"She's not that kind of person."

"I don't know her."

"Mattie…"

"No, Caleb. It's off the table. And it's Emma now."

Dan looks like he wants to argue, but he wisely says nothing. Brownie points to him.

Caleb sighs. "Sorry, I forgot."

"No big deal, but I am serious about the voodoo lady. She wants to explain to us how to do it, then you or Zeke can attempt it."

"You'd let me?" His eyebrows race toward his hairline.

"Well, yeah. You're family."

The dumbstruck look on his face is hilarious.

"What? You're Dan's brother. He's my family, so that makes you my family by default. Plus, you've proven you can be trusted."

He clears his throat and looks away. "Thank you."

"You're welcome."

"Do you guys have anything to eat? I

haven't eaten since lunch."

My stomach decides to voice its own opinion, and we all crack up. "No. I didn't think it was wise to have a lot of food on hand at the moment." Dan nods to me, and I stick out my tongue. "I think there are a few drive-throughs still open, though, like Wendy's and Sonic."

"I'm starved, so why don't I go grab us some grub? I think it'll be okay to feed the beast since she was only just infected. In a few days, we may need to start making her fast."

"Won't that make it worse?" I ask. "I mean, if we cut off all my food, won't that make the hunger worse?"

"Yes, the hunger will get worse, but the progress of the infection won't. It'll slow down a lot."

"You intend to starve me, don't you?"

They nod in unison.

"I hate you both."

My stomach grumbles in response.

While Caleb's gone, Dan takes a quick shower and comes back out in a pair of plaid pajama bottoms and a white t-shirt. The material stretches across his shoulders. "You been working out?"

He grins and flexes. "Can you tell?"

"You're getting ripped. I almost miss the old you."

"It's the sword. I think I've grown like five inches, and I've filled out. I'm stronger too. Caleb and I have been going to the gym to work off all the extra energy it gives me."

Dan's phone rings, and he picks it up off the dresser. "I thought you turned that off so Zeke wouldn't track you."

He shrugs. "You know your father. If he really wants to find us, turning off my phone isn't going to stop him. This is for you."

I catch the phone he tosses, and I grimace when I see who's calling. Zeke would be easier than this call.

"Hey, Mary."

"Oh, my God. Where are you? Your dad is out of his mind."

"I'm with Dan."

She pauses for a beat. "I figured that, but *where* are you?"

"Somewhere safe. I can't defend myself against random shades and ghosts in the hospital, so we left. I'm fine, I promise."

"Shades?" Her voice lowers. She doesn't like them, and I wonder if maybe Deleriel used them against her while he held her hostage.

"Yes, it came in while Nancy was in the room with me, but thankfully waited until she was gone to attack."

"Dang, girl. You do get into trouble."

Does everyone have to keep pointing that out?

"I have something I need to tell you."

"What?" she pauses for a heartbeat.

"Eric says hello."

"Caleb's here."

"What?" I don't have to see her to know the color has just drained from her face. Mary really liked Caleb. They had a thing before she was kidnapped, but when she came home, she wasn't in any shape for a relationship. Add that to Caleb choosing to follow in his father's footsteps in the family business of hunting instead of manning up and following his own dreams, Mary had to let him go. She needed someone strong enough to carry her while she was broken, and Caleb couldn't do that. He stayed with his family.

I didn't think it was fair, but I kept my mouth shut. His family had just lost Eli, and how was Caleb supposed to walk away from them when they needed him as much as she did? Sometimes life throws hard choices at us, and we make the decision that's best at the time, even if it feels like the wrong one.

"Dan called him for help, and he caught the first flight out. He's out getting food right now."

"I...how is he?"

"Good, I think. How are you?"

"I don't know. I didn't expect to see him, you know?"

"You don't have to."

"Please, girl, you think I'm letting you fight this thing by yourself? Not a chance. I'm here to help."

And that's why we're sisters. Maybe not blood sisters, but we are sisters where it counts. In our hearts.

"We're going to Bourbon Street tomorrow to visit a voodoo lady. Think you can skip class and come with? You and Eric?"

"Of course. Just text me the address, and we'll meet you there."

We talk a few more minutes before I let her go. "Think Caleb got lost? He's been gone a while."

"Maybe the first place he went to wasn't open." Dan crawls into bed beside me. "Your brother texted me too. How did he get my number?"

"I didn't give it to him." Leave it to Nathaniel to find a way to know everything about me.

"I told him what was going on, and he said he'd see what he could find out. I figured the more people we had looking for answers, the better."

Dan does *not* like my brother, but I can't blame him there. Nathaniel's family were the ones who originally made the deal with Deleriel to create a child whose power could open a doorway between Hell and Earth. Even Nathaniel thinks if his grandparents, my mother's family, find out what I can do, they'll kill me and take my gifts for themselves. He promised to keep my ability to bring images to life a secret. So far, he's kept that promise.

"When do you have to go back to Charlotte?" I ask and snuggle closer. I know he can't stay here indefinitely. He has work and school.

"I don't."

I spring up then hiss in pain.

He jerks up, alarmed. "Hey, now. Careful. You're going to start bleeding again."

"What do you mean, you don't have to go back?" Did he really just say that, or am I dreaming?

He grins. "I don't. I turned in my two weeks' notice the day I got back last month. Seeing you after months of being apart made me realize I can't do that again. I need to be here with you."

"But your mom…school…"

"I dropped out of UNC."

"You did what?" I screech so loud I know the neighbors are going to be calling the front desk.

He gives me this sheepish look that's meant to calm me but does anything but.

"You dropped out of college?"

"I'd already taken a leave of absence so I could be here with you after Deleriel, so I was behind when I went back. Then with all the stuff going on with Mom and work, I just couldn't keep up. Something had to give. I can always go back to school."

"You love forensic science, Dan. I don't want you to give that up."

"I love *you* more."

And all the anger drains out of me with those words.

"What about your mom's trial?"

"It got pushed back a little. The prosecutor had some kind of family emergency, and everything got rescheduled."

I scrub my face with both hands. "We still have to talk about this college thing."

He gives me a half-smile and pulls me back down so I'm lying curled up against him. "I already started looking for a school that has either a criminal justice or forensic science program close by. I'm going to try to start the spring semester."

"I don't know of any schools right off

that have forensic science down here." He loves that program.

"You know what I've learned since I dropped out of school?"

"What?" My teeth chew at my bottom lip. Why didn't he tell me he'd dropped out of college?

"When I started working full time as a cop and not worried about anything else, I discovered I love what I do. I used to think all I wanted to do was the forensic side, figure out what happened based on the physical evidence. But it's the mystery that I'm more drawn to. I want to know the why instead of the how. Does that make sense?"

It actually does. Dan is really good at being a cop. I always thought it would be a shame if he gave up being out there in the field to work in a lab. I know shows like *CSI* made forensic science cool, but Dan has the mind to be an exceptional police officer.

"Yeah, Officer Dan, it does."

"I'm not as concerned about finding a forensic program anymore. I do want my degree, though. It'll help me when I want to move up."

"Have you talked to the police department down here?"

He nods. "James knows some people in the upper brass. He didn't know I'd already applied and had set up an interview. I'm pretty sure he put in a call even though I asked him not to."

"Am I a bad person for not feeling guilty about you moving down here when the Malones moved to Charlotte so they could get to know you?"

"No, Squirt, you're not a bad person." His lips graze my temple, and a shiver works its way down my spine. "You need me as much as I need you."

"I do, you know. Need you." Looking up into those puppy dog eyes, I smile. "I never knew anyone could love me as much as you do, and I never thought I'd love someone the way I do you. I didn't think I was worth the effort."

"You are, though. It took me a long time to get past all those walls of yours, but I never gave up. Even when I kept telling myself to think of you as a little sister, I knew deep down you *were* worth the effort. I always knew this is where we'd end up, if I'm being truthful. I'm just sorry I hurt you."

"You did, but it was what it was. You love me, and that's what counts."

He kisses me again, and then we both settle down. He shoots Caleb a text.

"Where is he?" I ask around a yawn.

"He stopped to eat before coming back. He got you a double cheeseburger from Wendy's."

I shake my head. I would have stopped and scarfed food too, so I can't even be mad he's starving me.

"You think you'll be okay long enough for me to go to the vending machine and grab some drinks?"

"Yeah, I'm good. Everything is salted, and you even put up some warding. I'm snug as a bug."

"You're starting to sound southern."

"Well, I am southern."

He laughs and slides out of the bed. "I'll be back in a few minutes."

I relax against the pillows and close my eyes. I hear the door open and close, knowing I won't be alone for long. It doesn't matter, though, because I'm exhausted and am asleep within a matter of minutes, safe and content for the first time in days.

What did I do last night?

Groaning, I reach for the bottle of whiskey sitting on my desk, ignoring the tumbler that's still half-full of the fiery amber liquid. Unscrewing the lid, I wash out my mouth then take a strong swallow. The burn is delicious, even at this hour. I ignore the queasiness of my stomach and the walls spinning.

I must have passed out at my desk. But how did I get here? The last thing I remember is going out for drinks with some friends. We'd ended up in that new bar, not the one on Bourbon Street, but the one…

Shaking my head, I give up trying to think. I'm too hungover for this.

My eyes are sore and bleary, but then again, I haven't gotten this drunk in a long time. Stumbling my way to my bathroom, I wince when I see my reflection in the mirror. Rough doesn't even begin to describe how I look.

No more shots for me any time soon.

Getting in the shower, I let the heat relax stiff muscles. Falling asleep at the desk is not good for me. Age has crept up, and with it, the aches and pains I never would have thought I'd be subjected to.

Why didn't Nicki wake me up? She was probably pissed I went out and got hammered. It's not like I do it all the time. Two kids and a mortgage keep me responsible, but it's good to let loose sometimes. I wish she'd realize this. We used to go out every Saturday and just have fun.

Not that I'm complaining. I love my wife and my kids. They're everything to me. Still, a little dose of fun never hurt anyone.

Once I'm out of the shower and dressed, I jog downstairs. It's after two in the afternoon. The kids are probably out back playing, with Nicki sitting at the patio table, reading one of her romance novels I call soft porn in print. That woman loves her books. She has more than she can realistically get through, and still she buys more.

It's quiet. The lights are off. How didn't I notice that when I ran upstairs earlier? Maybe she and the kids went out since I was passed out drunk? It's not like her to not leave me a note. She might be angry, but she'd still leave a note telling me where she'd gone.

Checking the kitchen and the office again, I scratch my head. Still no note. The whiskey bottle calls to me, but I pick up the tumbler this time and toss back what's left in that. Worry gnaws at me. I hope she didn't go out angry. Driving while mad can be just as dangerous as drunk driving. My brother died like that. Stormed out of the house after a fight with our parents and lost control of the car, wrapping it around a tree. Nicki

159

knows this. She knows how I feel about driving while emotional.

Perhaps she took the kids to the park or to get some ice cream. I'm being paranoid. Food will help to settle my nerves. My stomach has been growling since I woke up. Opening the fridge, I look inside, but don't really see anything I want. The kids' juice boxes and two gallons of milk are front and center. There's turkey, ham, and chicken for sandwiches, but I pass by that. My focus lands on a pack of hamburger. We planned on grilling out today. I'll get a jump start on the burgers while she's out.

Once I grab what I need, I take it all outside to the deck and set up the grill. It's charcoal. A lot of people prefer gas grills, but the burgers just don't taste the same. While the charcoal is heating, I go back inside to look for my phone. It's not on my desk or on the front hallway table with my keys.

Don't tell me I lost my phone last night. She really is going to kill me.

Then again, as drunk as I was, I could have put it anywhere. I go over to the kitchen counter and pick up the landline. Nicki insisted on it, saying you never know when it will come in handy. I thought our cells were enough, but she was right, as usual. The landline is indeed coming in handy. Punching in my phone number, I listen. Almost immediately, I hear it ringing.

Upstairs.

Great. I probably stumbled into the bedroom drunk, and she got pissed, threw me out, and I passed out downstairs in the office. I hope I didn't wake up the kids. No wonder she's not here. If I woke up the baby, she'll have my head. David hasn't been sleeping. The poor baby has colic. We've both been up with him more nights than I care to count.

Feeling like an idiot, I make my way upstairs. When the phone stops ringing, I call it again. Traveling along the hall, I hear it down at the end, in the baby's room. Yeah, Nicki is probably pissed. There's no way I didn't wake Davey up if my cell is in there. No wonder she's not here. She's probably so mad, I'll be lucky to not get kicked to the couch for the next month.

My footsteps falter when I flip on the hallway light. There's something on the carpet. Going closer, I let out a little hiss of surprise. It looks like a bloody footprint. My eyes travel the path of the footsteps. They're up and down the entire hallway. What…?

Without thinking, I rush into the baby's room. Blood is everywhere. On the walls, on the carpet, on the furniture. On the crib.

No.

Running, I come to a stop at the crib and look down.

What is left of my son laughs at me. His stuffed giraffe stares up at me, the brown eyes glassy, the fur wet and sticky with Davey's blood. Bits and pieces of my son are scattered in the crib.

Backing away, my mind numb with shock, I turn and run to my daughter's room. The pink princess suite, my wife calls it. Trish is five and in love with all things princess. I had a princess castle built around her bed.

The doorknob is stained red.

No, no, no, no, no…

My hand shaking, I twist the knob and open the door.

My stomach heaves, and I vomit right where I stand.

My wife is on the floor, disemboweled.

My daughter is lying on her bed, her unseeing blue eyes staring at me.

I can't breathe. I can't think.

Grief tears at me, shreds me until there's nothing left.

What happened?

Why are they dead?

They're dead.

All of them.

How did I not see this last night?

Something tickles the back of my mind, a memory so stark and horrible, I deny it. But then I think about it.

Walking back into the master bedroom, I look at the open bathroom door.

It can't be true.

The open door taunts me, and I take a ragged breath.

I have to know.

The basket of bath toys is sitting by the tub, the little yellow ducky right on top.

Trish loves that thing. She insists the little baby duck needs water, and we find her in the bathroom all the time, filling up the sink so the ducky can play in the water.

Pain slices through my chest. She won't be filling up the sink anymore.

Closing my eyes, I try to push down all those feelings. I have to know.

Truth time.

I check the tub. There are red stains in the bottom.

My stomach heaves.

Earlier, I'd noticed the red water, but in my hungover, fuzzy mind, I'd dismissed it. There is no dismissing it now.

The hamper reveals clothes that are stained with dried blood. My shirt is covered in it.

Maybe I didn't do this.

Maybe I came home and saw it.

Maybe that's why I swallowed half a bottle of whiskey.

Hot liquid rushes, and I barely make the toilet before my stomach empties itself. Only what I see makes me even sicker, and I curl up on the bathroom floor, my brain unable to cope with what my eyes are seeing.

That can't be bits and pieces of my family in that toilet bowl.

The yellow ducky stares at me from where it's sitting on the throne of toys, its eyes accusing.

Dear God, what have I done?

"No!" I fight against the thing holding me. I can't be here. This isn't real. I can't see this.

"It's a dream, Mattie!"

Dan's shout is like a beacon on the darkest of nights, and I come out of the dream, seeking the safety of his arms. That wasn't just a dream.

That was a vision.

"Easy." He untangles the cover from around me. "You're okay. It was just a dream."

I throw myself at him, not ashamed of the tears. For once, I welcome them. What I'd just seen was horrific, something I will never be able to un-see. Something no one should ever have to see.

"What's wrong?" Caleb's sleepy voice only makes me cry harder. I don't know why, but it does.

"She had a nightmare, I think." Dan pulls me into his lap and rocks me. "It's okay. You're safe now."

The light flips on, and a bottle of water is shoved at me. "Here, drink this. It'll help."

My stomach heaves at the thought. "Bathroom," I whisper. "I need the bathroom."

Without a word, Dan picks me up and runs to bathroom. I'm barely on my knees in front of the toilet before I'm throwing up. Every single thing I'd eaten in the last couple hours comes back up. Thoughts of what had been in that toilet dance in front of me, and I start dry heaving.

"What's wrong with her?"

"I knew I shouldn't have let her talk me into discharging herself from the hospital. Her headaches are back."

"The seizures."

Dan nods miserably. "Come on, baby. Let's get you cleaned up, and then we're going back to the hospital."

"I…"

"No buts this time. You're sick."

I shake my head. "It's not a headache. It's…it's what I dreamed about."

Caleb squats beside me. "What did you dream about?"

"The roogie," I whisper and shove my fist in my mouth to keep from screaming. I want to shout, to scream, to cry at the horror of what I've just experienced.

"The Rougarou?"

I nod.

"Does she still have visions?" Caleb directs the question to Dan.

"I don't know…maybe? She hasn't said anything to me."

Normally, I'd get pissed at them for talking about me when I'm right here, but I can't. This has to be some form of shock.

Caleb rubs my back when I lay my head on the toilet seat. I'm drained. My nose wrinkles when the stench reaches me. Caleb reaches up and flushes it without me having to ask. He takes care of me as much as his brother does, but it's what his family does. The Malones were given the job of protecting living reapers. It's hardwired into his DNA to protect me.

"It was a vision."

"What did you see?" Dan takes up residence on the other side of me.

"I think I saw the man who turned into the roogie. It was awful."

"Did you see him change?"

"No." I curl up around the toilet. How to tell them what I saw?

"Did you see him feed?" Caleb asks quietly.

"Not exactly. I saw what was left of his family when he woke up. He didn't know. I felt everything. All of it. His worry when they weren't there, his love for them, and then when he saw the half-eaten bodies..." I shudder. God, I want to un-see that.

"You didn't see him do it, though?" Dan pulls my hair out of my face so it won't fall into the toilet.

"I saw what he threw up. I felt his horror and the pain…"

"He threw up partially digested pieces of human flesh, didn't he?"

I nod in response to Caleb's question.

Both men are quiet. What can you say to something like that?

After a few minutes, I hear the sink turn on, and then Dan is back with a cold washcloth, wiping my face. "Come on, Squirt. Let's get you cleaned up and back to bed." I don't say a word when he washes my face then picks me up, cradling me against his chest.

The blankets are pulled back, and he climbs in, never bothering to put me down. I don't want him to. This is my safe haven, and he knows it.

"If I can draw his face, can you run it through the police database?" Now that some of my shock is wearing off, my mind is beginning to play catch-up, and I know this is our best shot at finding the roogie before he hurts anyone else…or me.

"I'm not affiliated with any police department right now, Mattie." Dan keeps up the steady stroking of my hair, and that calms me down even more. "I don't have access."

"Neither do I. Maybe I can email it to Dad? He should be able to run it through some databases, but I'm not sure how long it will take. He's on another case right now in Missouri."

"I'm changing my major," I mutter. "I'm learning computers so we can hack the things we need."

"That is not funny," Dan says, clearly exasperated.

"Uh, I don't think she was being funny." Caleb sits on the bed and pulls his legs up so he's sitting Indian-style facing us.

"Of course, she is…" He finally looks at me then remembers I am not afraid to brush up against the opposite side of the law. "Tell me you're not serious."

"I could tell you that, but it would be a lie, and we did promise never to lie to each other. You really want me to break that promise, Officer Dan?"

He mutters something I don't quite catch, and Caleb laughs. "At least she's honest."

"Do you have Cass's number?" I could call him myself, but that opens up the possibility of having to return any number of voice mails and messages my father will have left me.

"Yeah, why?"

"Call him and see if he can get access to a police database. He may know a few local cops who can help."

Caleb gets up and rummages through his jeans, pulling out his phone before coming to sit back on the bed. If Zeke could see me now, sitting in a bed with two half naked men, he'd be fit to be tied, foaming at the mouth mad. Thank God he will never know.

"Hey, man, it's Caleb. You got a sec?"

"Put it on speakerphone." Dan pulls me in tighter, wrapping the blankets around me. I'm shivering. I didn't notice, but he did.

"Yeah, that's Dan. I'm here with him and Mat...er, Emma."

"Hi, Cass. How ya feeling?"

"I'm home, so better den I was."

"I have a question for you. If I can get

you a sketch of someone, do you know anyone in NOPD who can run it through some databases to identify the guy?"

He lets out a sigh. "I wish, *chèr*. Hunters and police doan get along. Dey doan like us poking around where we doan belong."

"Well, that sucks."

"Not everyone has an Officer Dan," Caleb points out, earning him a glare from Dan. "In all honestly, it's not like you see on TV. We can't just flash a fake badge and wing it to real officials. They're not as gullible. It's a lot harder for the hunter working alone or in teams to get information. If Dad weren't on the spook squad of the FBI, we'd really be hindered in trying to protect people from the more dangerous of the supernatural creatures out there."

"We need someplace for all the hunters to be able to go, to get resources and information. We need to work together with the police."

"We?" Caleb quirks a brow.

"She be a hunter too."

"What?" Dan's low growl is enough to

make my hair stand on end.

"No, I'm not. I help out here and there. Doesn't make me a hunter."

"You did say 'we,'" Caleb reminds me.

"We need to get her a real hunter's kit," Cass goes on. He can't see the glowering face of my boyfriend or the concern in Caleb's expression. "Girl's flashlight was so weak, it wouldn't even cut through more den ten feet in front of her."

"What good does a sketch do, then?" I fiddle with the blanket, trying to look anywhere but at the accusing eyes above me. He's pissed. I knew he would be when he figured out what I've really been doing. But Zeke was right. I help people; it's what I'm good at.

"A sketch?"

I tell him about my vision, and he's quiet for a long time while he digests one more weird thing about me. "You have visions?"

"Sometimes."

"Well, even if we can't get an ID from de police, it may still help us. We can use it to do a few searches ourselves, like

Google. De image might bring up his social media, at de very least."

I hadn't thought of that, but it's a good idea.

"That's a good idea." Dan echoes my thought. "Her drawings are so detailed it shouldn't be that hard for Google to pick up on the similarities."

"*Oui*, she's good," Cass agrees. "I saw one of her pictures de other day. I was shocked at how good she was."

Dan's smile is indulgent, despite how angry he is. He loves to hear people sing my praises over my art. "Have you seen the work she's done for her YouTube channel?"

"YouTube channel?" Caleb looks up, startled. "You're doing a YouTube channel?"

"Not my idea. Mary decided we need to do one."

"Mary?" He cocks his head. "You guys doing a fashion channel or something?"

I burst out laughing. "Do I look like a fashion kind of girl?"

He grins. "Not one bit. I don't think you'd brush your hair if people didn't pester you to do it."

True, I probably wouldn't.

"You remember that wannabe ghost hunter group I was telling you about? The one with the guy she had a crush on?"

He nods.

"Well, she got the idea from him. She thinks we should do our own ghost show."

Caleb winces, knowing exactly how I feel about being The Ghost Girl. I hate it. "You agreed to that?"

"Do you think I had a choice?" I shake my head. My sister is downright scary when she decides to go after something, and God help you if you're the obstacle in her way.

"Knowing your sister, no." Caleb smiles lazily. "She can be quite stubborn."

"Cass, I'll call you back tomorrow. I need to do the sketch, and then we're going to meet Caleb's voodoo lady too. She has an idea of how we might be able to track the curse back to its source."

"Really?"

"Yeah, we'll call you when we know more. Talk soon." I hang up on him before he can say anything else. A yawn overtakes me, and the thought of sleep is too much. I tense. No sleeping tonight, not if I'm going to dream about the roogie and more of his midnight snacking. "Caleb, can you grab the hospital bag over by the door? It has my sketchpad and pencils in it." Thank God for Nancy. Had she not brought that stuff by, I wouldn't have what I need to get this drawing done.

"We need to talk about the whole hunting thing."

I knew he wasn't going to let it go.

"Aren't you the one always trying to get me into police work?"

"Safe, normal, *legitimate* police work."

"Dan, you can walk up on a traffic stop and the driver shoot you dead. Normal police work is no different than hunting. We both track down clues and solve mysteries. I just chose to do it outside the police force. Where there aren't so many rules that get in the way."

"Rules are good. They keep you safe."

I take the bag from Caleb. "Sometimes, but sometimes you have to break the rules to save people."

Dan looks ready to argue, but I catch Caleb shaking his head out of the corner of my eye. "Why don't we table this discussion for now? Let her work on her drawing before the memory fades?"

Dan frowns but finally nods, reading something in his brother's expression I can't see. Must be brother or man-speak. Either way, I don't care, as long as it postpones this fight. I need to get these images out of my head before they take root and haunt me forever.

We go to meet Mary and Eric for breakfast at a little diner next to the university. I'm nervous for Caleb and Mary. They haven't seen or spoken to each other in over a year. I know Mary was mad at him even before she got kidnapped and dragged off to Hell, and Caleb was doing what Caleb does best, being the good son who pleases his parents.

What I didn't expect is for Nathaniel to be parked outside the diner when the three of us pull up. "Did you call him?" I ask Dan.

"Yesterday, but I told you about that.

He didn't say anything about coming down here."

"Who's that?" Caleb asks curiously as we get out of Dan's rental.

"My brother."

Aleric Nathaniel Buchard. He looks like me, with hazel eyes and dark brown hair. We even have the same shaped forehead, although his is a little wider than mine, him being a guy and all.

Caleb visibly tenses. He knows exactly who my brother is. A Dubois. The name is enough to terrify anyone in the supernatural world. I'm double cursed, really. My father is a Crane, and my biological mother is a Dubois. The two most hated families because of how dangerous they are. The Dubois family has done things not even my father would consider, though.

"He's not going to whip out some demon curse and throw at you." I slap Caleb in the middle and go to greet my brother.

He gives me a grin when I reach him. "Can't stay out of trouble, can you?"

"Why does everyone ask me that?" I

mutter.

"Because it's true?" Nathaniel hugs me, albeit carefully. We're growing on each other. It's not that instant family connection I had with Zeke. It's more like the one I have with my grandparents. I'm guarded. I don't trust Nathaniel. I want to, but I just don't. Only time will improve our relationship.

"You look like you tangled with a bear and lost."

"How did you know we'd be here?" I ask instead of snarking back at him.

"We share the same blood, Emma. I did a simple family locator spell this morning. I stopped at the hospital first, and then I checked with your father to see if you were there. He wouldn't say, but I got the feeling he didn't know any more than I did about your whereabouts. You were pulling out of the hotel parking lot when the spell led me to you, and I decided to follow. I was hoping you'd be headed for food. I'm starved."

"Family locator spell?" I ask as Dan and Caleb joins us.

"Blood calls to blood. It's an easy one

to learn. I'll teach you."

"Nathaniel, you remember Dan, and this is his brother, Caleb Malone."

"Malone?" I see the way Caleb's gaze sharpens, and an uneasy feeling wiggles around in my gut. "Any relation to James Malone?"

"He's our father," Dan tells him, a frown beginning to form. His instincts are kicking in, same as mine.

And this is why I can't simply trust Nathaniel. I don't know him, and I can't tell if his interest is because he's up to no good or simple curiosity based on family dealings with the FBI agent.

"I know him." Nathaniel opens his car door and pulls out several books and a laptop. "Come on, let me show you what I found."

His deep southern drawl has attracted the attention of several college girls. They giggle as he passes by, their eyes batting to beat forty. I roll mine and mutter the word *idiots* as I pass them. Dan chuckles, but the girls don't appreciate my sarcasm. They give me dirty looks as we search for a table.

"We need a bigger table," Caleb decides, "especially if Eric and Mary are joining us."

"Your sister is coming?" The obvious interest in Nathaniel's tone sets my teeth on edge, but he's been nothing but nice to her even though Mary's been nasty to him. I think he gets she's only trying to protect me. Admires it, even. I just hope he doesn't get any ideas about trying to hook up with my sister.

Then I grin.

No, I change my mind. He should try. Mary will put him in his place faster than I ever could.

Speak of the devil, and so shall she appear. The two of them walk into the diner, and I can immediately tell she's taken some extra time with her appearance even though she's trying to look like she's not in those hot pink sweatpants and loose flowy tank top shirt that's not really a tank top. Her long blonde hair is piled in a messy bun on the top of her head, and a pair of sunglasses are pushed up on her head like she's been driving and shoved them up there. Her makeup is flawless, and she looks more put together than half the girls in here who'd spent hours trying.

This is why Caleb thought she was doing a fashion channel. The girl loves clothes and makeup.

"Wow, you really did call in the cavalry," Mary says, coming over to hug me.

"Not me. Dan did."

Her gaze shifts to Caleb then lands on my brother. "Why is he here?"

The hostility in her voice is enough to raise eyebrows. "Because he's trying to help."

Her lip curls up in a snarl. She and Nathaniel are like oil and water. They don't mix well.

"Hathaway." Eric pries me away from Mary so he can look at me. "Girl, what am I gonna do with you? Don't you know better than to check yourself out of the hospital against medical advice?"

"Pfft," I wave him off after a hug, "I'm fine."

"You don't look fine." The brutal honesty in his words is telling. Eric is blunt. To a fault, sometimes. "You look like the dog chewed you up and spit you out the other end."

"Eww." Mary and I both gag at the visual. "That is gross."

"Good one." Dan bumps his fist with Eric.

"Boys are stupid," Mary agrees with a nod.

"Hello, Mary."

Caleb's soft greeting freezes her in place. Slowly, she turns her head to look at him. There's a flash of something in her eyes I don't have words for, but it's there and gone so fast, unless you were looking, you'd never have seen it. I know Caleb did. He was looking right at her.

"Caleb." Her voice is just as soft.

"Why don't we shove two of these tables together?" Eric suggests when the silence grows awkward.

"Good idea." He and Dan look around and find some empty tables in the back and set about doing just that. The waitress doesn't seem to mind. It's a morning hangout for the college kids. She's used to this kind of thing.

My brother beats Caleb to the open seat next to Mary. I am on her other side. It earns him a glare from Caleb, but he ignores it. He whispers something to Mary, and she makes a face but doesn't demand he move. I think she was worried Caleb might try for the seat, and she'd rather deal with Nathaniel than her feelings for Caleb.

Once everyone's order is placed and juice and coffee sit around the table, Dan tells them about last night, and I fill in the gaps. Nathaniel simply watches and listens the whole time. Unlike me, he's not a hothead. He doesn't rush in. He plots and plans every little detail. It's why he's going to make a very good attorney, something else I discovered about him. He started law school this year. He's skipping classes he can't afford to miss to be here.

And that says a lot.

It's the only reason I haven't let that bad feeling in my gut demand answers. He's here for me, and for a foster kid, that means more than anything else.

"So, this voodoo lady you are going to,

what does she think she can do?" Nathaniel sips at his orange juice, something else we both love.

"She thinks she can track the curse back to the caster."

Nathaniel puts his juice down and nails Caleb with eyes colder than the bitterest winter day. "There's only one way to do that. Some hack is not getting her hands on my sister's blood."

"She not a hack." Caleb returns the cold stare with one of his own. "She's helped us out more times than I can count. I trust her."

"Then you're a fool," he drawls. "Never trust a spellcaster."

Before an argument breaks out, I stop it in its tracks. "I already told him I wouldn't give her my blood."

Nathaniel nods, relieved. "I found a few things myself, things you're not going to like, but they do work."

"Black magic?"

His nostrils flare. "There is nothing wrong with using black magic when it's necessary."

"It leaves a stain on the soul." I can see

auras. I usually mute it, but one of the first things I'd noticed about my brother was all the black stains on his. Most likely from use of black magic.

"Everyone has a little darkness in their soul."

"Not all of us." Caleb's clipped reply is telling. He's sitting across from us, seething. He can see Nathaniel's interest in Mary. Mary may be having none of it, but that's not the point. If it were up to Caleb, they'd still be together, but he wasn't what Mary needed. He might still not be what she needs. I don't know.

What I do know is we're not going to spend the rest of the day with this hostility. "Okay, enough is enough. Both of you get over yourselves. Mary doesn't want either of you, so snapping at each other isn't helping anyone. We came here to figure out the roogie, and that's it."

"Roogie?" Nathaniel chokes on his juice. "You did not just call that beast a roogie?"

"Whatever." I shrug it off. "The point is we have a lot to do and not a lot of time to do it. No more fighting, hostile looks, or petty snarking."

"Wow, did you, the queen of snarking, just demand no more snarking?" Eric asks after a beat of shocked silence.

"Yes. The queen has declared it, and so shall it be."

Dan leans over and kisses my temple, whispering so only I can hear. "Thank you."

He doesn't like yelling at his brother, especially after losing Eli. I did it for him, and he's grateful. I did it for me too. I do not want another headache starting. He'd rush me to the hospital.

"Now, Nathaniel, what is in all those books you've piled on the table?"

"I flew into Georgia last night so I could raid my grandparents' study before coming here. They have several books on the Rougarou. As you know, it's a curse that causes an individual to turn more animal than human. A hunger drives them until they go mad."

I nod. We know this already.

"The curse is driven by hunger, need, insatiability."

"Are you trying to say the curse came

about because someone couldn't keep it in their pants?" Mary asks.

"I wouldn't have put it so crassly, but essentially, yes. This man was most likely cursed either by his wife…"

"No. He killed her."

"You know who it is, then?" His eyes light up. "This will be much simpler."

"No, I don't know who he is."

"Then how…"

"I have visions. I saw him and what he did to his family."

Nathaniel's face pales. "You saw…"

"Not the actual eating," I hurry to explain. "Just the aftereffects, what was left."

"I am so sorry. No one should see something like that."

"It is what it is. I can't stop the visions any more than I can stop an oncoming train."

"If it wasn't his wife, then it had to be someone he'd spurned," Dan muses as the waitress comes over and starts handing out plates of food. Once she's gone, he continues. "Maybe an affair."

"No. He loved his wife. I *felt* how

much he loved her. He'd never have cheated. He'd hurt himself first."

"He did eat her," Nathaniel reminds me.

"But he didn't remember doing it. Once he realized what he'd done, it nearly killed him. I think the hunger drove out his rational mind, or he wouldn't have touched his family with harmful intent. I think it's probably someone who wanted him, but he rebuffed her. She got angry."

"That makes sense," Nathaniel agrees. "If she felt betrayed by his lack of interest in her, it would give her a reason to make him hurt the same way she was hurting."

Two college kids pass by our table, and I look around to make sure we're not drawing attention with our talk of cannibalism. No one in the diner even bats an eye at our conversation. It's New Orleans, after all. They're used to all things weird, paranormal, and voodoo.

"How is any of this going to help us, though?" Mary leans as far away from my brother as she can. If he notices, he doesn't say anything. I'm still not sure if her intense dislike of him is simply because of the way my grandparents described the Dubois family, or if it's something else. I make a mental note to chat with her about that.

"Everything helps." Dan pushes his food around on his plate, thinking. "Even the smallest detail can sometimes break a case wide open. We have an image of him, we just need to be able to run it through some police databases. I can't, since I'm no longer affiliated with a police force, and Caleb says he's not sure when James would have time."

"You need a hacker." Eric pulls his phone out and starts texting.

"Wait, you know someone who can hack the police computers?"

He gives me his most mischievous half-grin. "You know them too."

I know them? As far as I know, I don't know anyone who can hack a computer system. "Who?"

"You remember Jordan from the Ghost Chasers?"

"The kid who did all the computer

stuff?" My eyes widen. I do remember him. I hadn't really thought much about what else he could do other than rig up cameras to computers. He'd done all the computer stuff for the wannabe Scooby gang.

"One and the same. Turns out he's in my fraternity."

Mary lets out a sigh. Eric rushed a frat house, and now it's all he talks about. Mary may stuff his head in the toilet before all is said and done.

"Which one?" Nathaniel asks curiously.

"Alpha Omega." He stuffs a whole piece of bacon in his mouth. "Best one on campus."

"You only think that because it's the one you're in."

"No, he's right." Nathaniel picks up his coffee and takes a sip. "It is the most prestigious one on many campuses across the US."

She's not buying what he's selling.

He shrugs. "Believe it or not. It's the one I belong to."

"Really?" Eric perks up, taking interest

in the conversation.

Nathaniel nods. "Best frat on campus."

The two of them make some kind of weird symbol with their hands and burst out laughing.

Mary and I exchange a disgusted glance. Frat boys.

"We're off topic." Caleb pushes his pancakes to the side and digs into his bacon and eggs. "You were telling us you might have a way to stop the Rougarou?"

"Yes," Nathaniel drawls. "Y'all just distracted me."

"Y'all?" Mary is taken aback. "I thought slang was above you."

"Nah." He takes a long drink of his coffee. "I'm not nearly as genteel as my grandparents. I'm not as stuffy as them either."

"But you are as dangerous."

All eyes swivel to Caleb at that little comment.

Nathaniel grins in a way that would send the devil running, and I shiver. "No, I'm not. I'm more dangerous than either of them."

And he had to go and say it.

"Before they decide to take you out back and dispose of the body, care to tell us what you found out that can actually help us?" I attempt a joke, but it falls flat. No one really trusted him to begin with, and now every bit of cred he'd earned with them just went out the window with that little outburst.

He pulls the middle book out. "This works only if we find him. It will mean you don't have to kill him yourself."

That earns us a few curious glares.

"We're working on a screenplay," I tell the table beside us. "Going through some old books to make it more authentic."

They nod and go back to eating. Thank God Tulane has a film major.

"I'm not sure this is something you'd be willing to do, though," Nathaniel admits. "It requires essentially passing the curse on to someone else."

"You mean transfer it from me to them?"

He nods. "Exactly that. It's the least bloody of the three methods I have."

"No, I won't do this to anyone else." I push my empty plate away and pull

Mary's to me. She's only eaten about half of it; her attention keeps drifting to Caleb. He can't keep his eyes off her either. I wish those two would work, I really do, but I don't think it's gonna happen. At least not any time soon. They both still need to grow up. A lot. And I know that sounds ridiculous coming from me, but it is what it is.

"That's what I thought." He picks up one of the other two books. "This is messier, but at least it doesn't involve an innocent."

Once he's flipped the book to the correct page, he passes it over to me. An image of a man-like beast with the word Rougarou above it stares at me. They go into detail about the curse and then list a few ways to combat it, should you be infected. Death of the original Rougarou at the infected's own hands is listed first. We knew that. The only other option is a demon curse made by one of the first demons of Hell. I've dealt with one of the first demons. They're Fallen Angels. Slamming the book, I give it back to him. Nathaniel doesn't really know my history, but he knows I went up against a Fallen Angel and barely survived. Everyone in the paranormal community knows this.

"Why would you even show me that?" The low anger simmering in my voice startles everyone.

"Because it's a viable option, and since you did survive the last one…"

"The price I paid for that victory wasn't worth it. People were hurt, Nathaniel. People *died*." My gaze shifts to Mary. "No. That option is out of the question."

Nathaniel wants to argue, but he wisely shuts up and opens the third book. "You will not like this, but it's guaranteed to work."

This time as I read, I'm not immediately thrown back into a world of terrifying memories. This little passage is enough to give me terrors for the rest of my life. It's telling me how to make a demon curse myself from the blood of innocents.

"Absolutely not." I feel like throwing the danged book at his head.

"It works," he argues, just as stubborn as I am, "and you wouldn't have to go find the thing and get yourself killed trying to stop it."

"It requires the blood of a newborn baby!" I hiss. "I am not going out and killing a baby."

Mary lets out a shocked gasp, and all the men at the table lean forward, ready to thrash him.

"Nowhere in that text does it say you have to kill them, only blood them."

"And that's any better?" My eyes widen at the ridiculousness of having this argument over pancakes and bacon with a bunch of college kids listening in.

"Yes." He slams his hand down on the table. "Look at you. You're barely able to stand up. How are you going to fight one of those things in your condition?" His gaze swivels to Dan. "Why would you let her? She's going to get herself killed."

"Let me?" I stand, my body so sore I can barely move, but I push all that pain away and focus solely on my brother. "No one lets me do anything. Anyone who thinks they can tell me to jump and expect me to ask how high can just get off their high horse. I am not anyone's puppet. I am my own person. I make my own decisions and live with the consequences of my actions."

"And what about Dan?" Nathaniel counters. "Your actions don't just affect him, they determine if he lives or dies. You being stubborn is not only going to get yourself killed, but him as well."

Rage flashes to life inside of me, and heat suffuses every pore.

He did not just say that to me.

Before I can say or do anything, Dan is up and hustling me out of the diner. I tear my arm free and turn, intent on going back inside and letting Nathaniel have it.

"Stop, Mattie."

I shake my head, too angry to even speak.

"Your eyes are black."

I don't care. I take two steps toward the door, and he encircles me with his arms. The need to fling him off is strong, but if I do, I might hurt him, and he knows that is the one thing I will never do.

"Calm down." Dan pulls me with him to the rental car and shoves me inside. "You can't let him get to you like that. He was goading you."

"It worked."

"I know." He shuts the car door then goes around to get into the driver's side. Before he starts the car, he leans over and buckles me in himself.

He doesn't take me back to the hotel. Instead, we drive a little way out into the country toward where some of the older plantation homes are. We're both quiet until he turns down an old dirt road.

"Where are we going?"

"To a place."

"Duh, but what place?"

His eyes twinkle with laughter. "You'll see."

Some of my rage drains away, replaced by curiosity. Where are we going?

A lake.

That's where we end up. Dan brought me to the shell of an old abandoned plantation whose property houses the most gorgeous lake I've ever seen. The clearing we're in is surrounded by wildflowers. The sky above is a clear and bright blue, not a cloud to mar its beauty.

"This is beautiful." I twirl around, looking at everything.

"Easy, there. You're going to hurt yourself." Strong but gentle hands catch me and pull me to him. "If you break any of those wounds open, you'll be sorry later."

"It'll be worth it." I smile up at him, every ounce of rage fluttering away in the wind. "Thank you for bringing me here."

"You're welcome." He leads me over to the water's edge and sits, pulling me into his lap so our feet are hanging off the edge of the bank down toward the water.

"Wait, there aren't any gators out here, are there?"

"Maybe."

"Dan!" He knows I'm terrified of one sneaking up on me and taking a chunk of flesh or two.

"I'll keep you safe from the wild animals." His breath tickles my ear, and another shiver goes down my back.

"You always keep me safe."

"And I always will."

That promise might seem ordinary to a lot of people, but for us, it's the most basic truth. We keep each other safe. We protect each other even when it costs us the most. It's why he's my home.

Leaning back, I settle against his broad chest. "I almost hurt him."

"I know. It's why I got you out of there."

"Caleb…"

"Mary and Eric will give him a ride. I gave him my keycard earlier because I'd planned on bringing you out here after breakfast."

"I don't think being around each other is good for them."

"Or maybe it's exactly what they need," he counters. "Caleb loves her."

"Mary likes him, I know that much, but she needs someone who can put her first, and I don't think Caleb can."

"They'll work it out or they won't." His lips graze my earlobe, and my eyes drift shut.

"I guess," I whisper, lost in the sensations stirring up a storm inside. Old ones and new ones. I've loved Dan for so long, but it's only recently I've let that love manifest physically. For the longest time, I thought we'd just be friends because he kept pushing me away, saying I was too young, and then he was with Meg. Then Eli happened, and I was so confused. But once I made up my mind, it's like my body took over and said, "Ha, you finally figured it out. Now let me

203

show you what we've been missing!"

Stupid hormones.

"How did you find out about this place?" I ask as his lips travel down my jawline.

"Mrs. Banks told me about it. I told her I wanted to take you somewhere special, but I didn't know the area."

Mrs. Banks, my father's housekeeper, is a peach of a woman. I love her even more for sending us out here.

"I have to remember to do something extra nice for her." I roll my head to look up at him. "Do you think Nathaniel provoked me on purpose?"

He's quiet for a full minute while he thinks. "No. I honestly don't. He seems to care about you."

"But…"

"But I still don't trust him."

"Me either. It's awful, I know, but I just don't."

"He makes it hard to trust him." Dan lifts me slightly so he can get more comfortable. "It's the way he is, that gleam in his eyes. Like when he was talking about knowing James. It set off every internal alarm I have. I told Caleb to ask James about Nathaniel."

"I got the same hinky feeling," I confess. "Part of me wants to believe it's just how he is, like Eric's a born flirt. Nathaniel is…he likes to shock people and instigate trouble."

Dan's hands tighten where they're resting on the tops of my thighs. "I don't think it's as simple as that."

"I know, but he's my brother. I don't want to believe his grand scheme is to hurt me or anyone I love."

"That's because you're a good person, Squirt. You don't want to believe the worst in people even though that's what you've seen most of your life. That's part of why I love you so much. There's an inherent kindness buried beneath all those layers of sarcasm you shield yourself in. Not many people get to see that side of you, but I do. I saw it even when you didn't want me to. You're beautiful, Mattie, inside and out."

Hormones.

On steroids.

That's what his words do to me.

Heck, they might even have burst an ovary.

"I…"

"Shh." He stops me by putting a finger to my lips. "Just listen, okay?"

I nod, unsure of where he's going with this.

"When we go back to Charlotte for my mom's trial, I want you to remember this, to remember how I feel about you. I don't want you to let her anger and what she may or may not say to you ruin this right here. Promise me you won't let her run you off. I wish I could protect you from her hatred, that I didn't need you there…"

It's my turn to shush him. "Dan, she's your mother, and you love her. She's always going to be your mother, and she will always look out for you and try to protect you and Cameron. She loves you. Every single thing she's ever said or done to me, I take with a grain of salt because I know why she's doing it. No one's running me off. In it for the long haul, remember?"

His smile is stunning.

"I bought you a ring."

"What?" He did not just say that.

"I know you're not ready for it yet. It may be years before you're ready for it. But I saw it, and I knew it was perfect. It's in my underwear drawer at home."

He bought me a ring.

He told me he was going to marry me one day, that he'd wait until I was ready.

He bought a ring.

"Mattie?" His voice is whisper soft.

"Hmm?"

"How freaked out are you?"

"On a scale of one to ten...fifty."

He laughs. "I'm not giving it to you today, but when you're ready, it's waiting."

Movement out of the corner of my eye catches my attention. Turning, I see a woman standing there, watching us. Her long brown hair is mussed, she has a split lip, and she's cradling her left arm. She's wearing a nightgown that went out of style over a hundred years ago.

Why?

Why do freaking ghosts have to ruin our moment?

I hate them some days.

"What's wrong?" Dan whispers.

"Ghost," I whisper back, trying not to draw her attention.

"I didn't even think," he mutters. "Of course, there'd be ghosts here. It's an old plantation."

"It's okay." I pat his hand. "I was hoping we'd get longer before they started climbing out of the woodshed."

"Climbing out of the woodshed?"

"I heard it on TV, okay?" Heat steals over my cheeks. He's been teasing me about all the southern colloquialisms I've picked up.

"I love you." He bends to press a quick kiss to my forehead.

"Me too."

"You love you too, huh?" He grins, and I can't help but laugh. He's such an idiot sometimes.

"Sure do, but not nearly as much as I love you." Twisting slightly, I pull his head down to mine and kiss him with all the emotion I can't put into words.

The sound of splashing water brings me crashing back to reality. I pull away from Dan and look toward the lake. Several bloated corpses are treading water, heading right for us.

"It's time to go," I say, my gaze fixed on their steady approach.

"A lot of them?" Dan pushes off the ground, keeping me locked against him. Not sure how he manages, but he does.

"Yes."

He swings me up into his arms, and I fight back the need to shout from pain. I'm in more pain today than I've been since I woke up in the hospital a couple days ago. Once we're in the car, he opens the glove box and hands me my medicine bottle. The doctor prescribed me extra-extra strength ibuprofen when I refused pain meds. I shake out two and swallow them with the water he hands over.

"You should have told me you were hurting." The accusation in his eyes is harsh.

"We got stuff to do, Officer Dan. My being in pain isn't going to stop the clock on our timeline. Eight days to figure out how to stop the roogie, or Cass and I die. Pain is secondary to that."

He gives me one of his patented Officer Dan looks.

"Let's go get Caleb and meet his voodoo lady. I don't want to resort to making a newborn bleed."

He shakes his head, just as disgusted as I am by that thought.

But he doesn't argue with me. Instead, he puts the car in gear, and I glance behind us at all the ghosts gathered where we'd just been sitting.

Some days I really hate them.

Even as I want to help them, I hate them.

Dan texted Caleb and Nathaniel to meet us on Bourbon Street. Thanks to the handy dandy GPS, we didn't get lost. Had I been driving, we'd probably still have gotten lost. I am not good with directions. My first couple weeks driving around down here, I constantly got lost. Since Dan had a front row seat for all of that, he now refuses to let me drive.

I can't blame him.

Plus, I'm in no shape to drive today. I hurt too much.

What I haven't told him is that the hunger gnawing at my gut is starting to get unbearable. I know I just ate a few hours ago, but it feels like I haven't eaten in days. Thirst is starting to become a factor. I drank his water and mine in less than three minutes. Anything, really, to fill up my stomach and ease the hunger growing there.

Dan parks the car, and we walk slowly up the street to the voodoo shop, La Rou's. I snort at the name. It's close to Rougarou. Maybe it's fate's way of saying she'll have an answer for me.

Caleb, Mary, Eric, and Nathaniel are already in the shop when we arrive. No one's killed each other yet, so I'm counting that as a win.

The place is exactly what I imagined. Dark wood shelves, rows upon rows of bottled herbs and other things I don't want to think about. There's even a sign for livestock. I know voodoo requires a blood sacrifice for some of their work, but to sell poor animals right here? I shudder at the thought.

Nathaniel comes over as soon as he sees us. "I'm sorry. I didn't mean to upset you earlier. I let my anger get the better of me."

"Why were you so angry?"

He sighs and runs a hand through his hair. It's longer than the last time I saw him. He needs a trim.

"Because you're running around unprotected, almost getting yourself killed. I just found you. I can't lose you yet."

The raw emotion in his voice startles me. I thought I was more of a curiosity to him than family, but I'm not so sure right now.

"She's harder to kill than she looks." Dan's arms go around me, understanding I need some strength without me having to ask.

"I get that. I looked up everything to do with Mattie Hathaway. You're a survivor, but that doesn't mean you can't die. You don't know this world like I do. You didn't grow up in it, learn how to protect yourself against things you can't see coming. It's more than just ghosts and Rougarous. The supernatural world is lethal, and you're bouncing around in it without a care. It scares me you seem to have not one thought for yourself."

"You're really freaked out, aren't you?"

We all turn to see Mary standing to the side, listening.

"Why does everyone assume I'm cold and heartless?" His shoulders slump.

"Because you are?" Mary offers, but not unkindly.

"You're right, Mary. I am cold, and I am heartless to anyone who is not my family. She's my family. My blood runs through her veins. We may not have known each other long, but family means something to me. I protect what's mine, and she's mine. I won't let anyone hurt her if I can help it, even herself."

Mary regards him, her eyes unreadable. "You aren't planning to hurt her?"

"No!" he shouts, his anger finally breaking through.

"But you were going to." She keeps her voice as mild as his is harsh.

"I was." I'm shocked he admitted that. "I made up my mind to come here and steal her gifts. But then I met her, and this strange feeling bubbled up, something I can't even describe, and I knew I'd never hurt her. She's part of me, and I could no more hurt her than I would myself. When will you people understand that?"

"Maybe when you stop giving off your creepy vibes?" Mary says, turning to look at the items on the shelf she's standing next to.

"Creepy vibes?"

She nods. "You're creepy."

"That makes no sense."

"It does." She picks up a green glass jar. "What is *terre de cimetière*?"

"Cemetery dirt." Nathaniel smirks when she hastily sets it down.

"See, that's why you're creepy. You know what cemetery dirt is."

He cocks a brow. "Just because I speak French, I'm creepy?"

"It's more like the tone of your voice. You *know* what it's used for."

"I do," he agrees.

"See? Creepy."

Dan chuckles so low only I hear him. The two of them are downright funny. Caleb doesn't appear to think so, however. He's glaring holes into both of them. I feel like we're back in high school.

"Where is this voodoo lady of yours?" I ask to break some of the palpable tension in the room. Best get this done before Caleb murders my brother.

"Probably in the back. I'll go get her." Caleb stomps—yes, stomps—off toward the back.

"What is his problem?" Nathaniel asks.

"You're flirting with his girl," Eric drawls. I'd almost forgotten he was here.

"I'm not his girl," Mary denies.

"Yes, you are." Eric nods like that's the end of the conversation.

Mary's eyes narrow. "I might have been once, but he made his choice."

"He chose to stay with his family for support after they lost his brother." The quiet force in Eric's words is telling. He's blunt, and maybe Mary needs to hear this. "You expected him to abandon them days after Eli's funeral? He loves you, Mary, but they're his family. It wasn't fair to make him choose."

"I never asked him to choose."

"Not in so many words, but it was there."

Nathaniel remains quiet, and I know he's taking it all in for later dissection. Dan does this as well. It's what makes him a good police officer.

"None of us wanted to say anything," Eric goes on, "because of what you were going through, but enough is enough, Mary. That man loves you. Stop punishing him for being there for his family."

I want to clap, but I refrain. He's just told her everything I wanted to but was afraid to because of what her reaction might be.

Her face pales. "I didn't realize that's what I was doing."

"You didn't mean to." I pull away from Dan and grab her hands, squeezing gently. "You were hurting, and I don't think being around him in the beginning would have been good for you, but you're healing, Mary. I think you're ready to sit down and have a conversation with him. Figure out what you both want. If you want to move on, then tell him, or if you want to try again, then do that. Either way, I think it's time to get this sorted, yeah?"

She nods, her expression a mix of confusion and sadness. I don't think she ever really thought about what her actions meant to Caleb or even herself. She cut him off after Deleriel. He tried to call, to come see her. He texted. I told him to give her time, that she had to heal, and that's what he's done. She needs to figure out what she wants and either cut him loose or try again. Eric's right about that.

"When did you grow up, Em?"

"A long time ago."

She hugs me before turning back to the shop itself. "Enough of all this emotional baggage. Isn't this the coolest place ever?"

I arch a brow. She thinks this place is cool?

"Just think, we could use someplace like this for the backdrop to our opening. Way cooler than Wade's opening."

His name leaves a sour taste in my mouth. Wade is the head investigator for

The Ghost Chasers and Mary's first crush, post-Deleriel. She liked him, and I bit my tongue while they dated. Thank God they broke up not long after the investigation we helped with. That guy is a total douche.

"What are you talking about?" Nathaniel asks.

"Mary's bound and determined to start our own YouTube channel." This subject is the bane of my existence. I hate the very idea, but she's sunk her teeth into it and won't let go. Eric's not helping either. He's as excited as she is.

"That's...interesting."

That's one way of putting it.

I'm saved from answering when Caleb comes back out leading his voodoo lady. She's older than I thought, maybe in her fifties. She has on a white headdress, a stark contrast to her ebony skin. Her eyes are a warm brown, so light they could be deemed closer to amber. She's short and curvy.

Had she not been staring daggers at me, I would have said she wasn't just beautiful for a woman her age but dignified.

Hard to do that when someone's looking at you like they want to shoot you where you stand.

"How dare you bring this filth into my shop?"

Her words stop everyone in their tracks. All eyes turn to her, but hers never leave mine.

I am so sick of people judging me based on things I can't control. Like my demon blood. Dirty blood. I always think of it as dirty blood.

"Cherise, she's family."

Cherise, AKA the voodoo lady, turns to him, shocked. "You call that filth family?"

"This filth is standing right here." That darkness swells up, overtaking everything. The pain in my body recedes, and I welcome it. "You have no idea what I am, lady."

"I know who you are." Her lip curls up in disgust. "You're a Crane."

"I said you don't know *what* I am." I take three steps, bringing me within touching distance. "This filth is tired of people like you. If I were you, I'd watch my mouth."

She hisses and takes a step back, enticing all that darkness to reach out and touch her. My hand snakes out, cupping her cheek. "You can't run from me, *chèr*."

She lets out a little cry of pain caused by my touch. I know this, and my demonic side swells with pride. "Let's make a deal, shall we? You help us, and I'll forget your very rude manners."

"I don't make deals with demons."

I laugh and pull her closer. "*Chèr*, this place stinks of demons, so don't lie to a liar."

Her hands start to shake, and she tries to push me away, but my hand is fused to her skin. "Move, and you'll make me hurt you."

"Mattie." Dan's quiet voice is in my ear. "Let her go."

"No. She thinks I'm filth. She wants me to be a demon, I'll be a demon."

"That's not you talking, Squirt. It's the curse inside of you."

"That is her." Nathaniel steps up. "It's

the side of herself she keeps hidden, the side *she* hides from. The curse is feeding that darkness, though. The faster we find the Rougarou, the better. The more the demon half of her feeds off that curse, the stronger it becomes. We need to stop it before it consumes her."

Part of me knows he's right, but the other part of me wants this woman to suffer for insulting me. Wants her bleed, to cry out for forgiveness. She whimpers, and I see smoke start to curl up from beneath my fingers. I'm burning her skin. The shock is enough to force my hand away from her, and I stumble back. I want to be horrified, but deep down, I'm not. And that scares the daylights out of me.

There's a dark red burn in the shape of my handprint on her cheek. A smile tilts my lips. "Deal or no deal? You don't want to test me."

She lets out a shuddering breath. "Deal."

I smile, one full of teeth and reserved for people I hate. It's not nice.

"How do we track the person who cast

the curse?" Caleb asks, putting himself between me and Cherise. Not that I blame him. I still have the urge to hurt her.

Dan's arms go around me and pull me into his chest. I snarl, not wanting to feel anything associated with him. I want to hold onto my anger, to this need to hurt.

"Calm down," he whispers. His fingers knead the skin of my upper arms.

"Maybe you should take her and wait in the car?" Eric suggests. "She needs a cool-down."

"No. I want to hear this."

Dan picks me up and starts walking. I kick him in the shin. He grunts but keeps walking.

"I will make a scene right here and now if you don't put me down," I threaten.

"Go ahead." Eric rushes to open the shop door for us, and I do exactly what I threatened. I start shouting for him to put me down. People stare, several guys come over, but he warns them off with his eyes. It's the warrior the sword has made him. He can intimidate with only a look. He digs out his keys and puts me in the car, stopping to buckle my seatbelt.

Anger burns like a volcano ready to erupt, and when he gets into the passenger side, it takes everything I have not to give in to the urge to hit him. The urge to hurt him is all I need to start cooling down. Even the depraved demon side of me can't make me hurt him.

He sits there, his expression unreadable.

"I…" Blinking my eyes to clear them, I take several deep, shuddering breaths.

"It wanted me to hurt you," I finally whisper. "I wanted to hurt you."

"But you didn't."

Still not a drop of emotion from him. He should be mad. He should shout at me, blame me for the anger driving me. But he merely sits there.

"Are you mad?" I ask after a few minutes. "I kicked you."

"You did," he agrees.

"Aren't you mad at me for doing that?"

He shakes his head.

"Why?"

"Because that wasn't you in there."

"But Nathaniel…"

"He doesn't know you, not the way I do." He finally looks at me. "That, in there? That was a result of you not talking to me, to Silas, to your dad, to Mary and Eric. Hell, you could have even talked to Nathaniel about this, but you chose not to, Mattie. You chose to keep all that bottled up inside until you blew a gasket. I'm more disappointed in you than anything else."

It feels like he slapped me with the word "disappointed." And he's cussing. Dan never cusses. At least not around me.

"I understand you, Mattie Louise Hathaway, better than you understand yourself. You don't open up to people, you don't confess your deepest fears to just anyone. But we're your family. You can trust us. You can trust *me*. If you're struggling, then you need to tell me. I can't help you if I don't know something's wrong."

"I'm afraid." Something I keep buried so deep, even I didn't realize it was there bubbles up. "Everyone leaves me, Dan.

What if this darkness is the thing that makes you leave too? What if all this dirty blood in my veins is too much? What if you run?"

"Hey." He takes my face in both hands and makes me look at him. "I'm in this for the long haul, demon blood and all. I told you that once already. I meant it then, and I mean it now. What happened in there didn't scare me off, it just makes me more determined to help you through this, to make sure you come out the other side the same person you are underneath all that blackness. Your heart is bigger than anyone's I know. You forgave my mother when I haven't even been able to bring myself to do it."

"You haven't forgiven her?"

Pain lashes at me from his gaze. "I don't know how to forgive her."

All the darkness recedes, replaced by a love so deep, it scares me worse than the darkness slowly eating me alive.

"Dan."

He looks up, and my heart breaks for him. Here he is trying to comfort me and convince me he's not leaving, when he

226

needs the comfort more than I do. I lean over and growl when the seatbelt stops me. I unsnap it and crawl over the console to wedge myself into his lap.

"I am so sorry."

"For what?"

"For not realizing you needed me. It's okay not to forgive her. You can love her and not condone what she did. There's no law saying you have to do both."

"It hurts her, though," he confesses. "Every time I look at her, I can see how much it hurts her."

"That's okay too. No one has the right to tell you how to feel, not even your mother who loves you."

He buries his face between my neck and my shoulder. Wetness dampens my skin. I had no idea he was hurting this much. I guess dampening the bond between us cut me off from his inner emotions as much as it did him from mine. Maybe it wasn't such a good idea.

"I'm so sorry," I murmur. "I should have been here for you."

"No, you were dealing with enough stuff of your own. I had Dad and Cam to help me."

"And the Malones."

He nods. "Benny says to tell you he misses you."

Benny Malone is Dan's baby brother. He and I had gotten close last year while we'd been hidden at Silas's for months so I could get ready to face Deleriel. He'd ordered the man who'd been doing his bidding, a pedophile who enjoyed hurting children, to take Benny. Silas found him before anything bad could happen to the kid, something his entire family is grateful for even if that gratitude is aimed at a demon.

"I miss him too. I can't wait to see him and his Hellhound when we go back to Charlotte."

"You ready to tell me what that was all about in there?"

His shift in subjects isn't jarring. I expected it.

"My blood's dirty. Every single voodoo lady I've met in the last few days knows it. They've both told me I'm an abomination. I guess I just got sick of it, you know?"

He nods but waits me out, knowing there's more.

"What if they're right?"

"That you're filth, an abomination?"

"Yeah."

"Then I'm the king of Never-never land."

"What?" I laugh at his pious expression.

"You're not filth, sweetheart. You're not an abomination. You are unique and gifted, and you help people without thought to your own safety. Your brother's right about that. You jump in the fire to save someone who may not even deserve saving. If that's filth, then sign me up. I want some of it."

I smile and lean forward to kiss him, only to stop and double over in pain. My shoulder is on fire, and every muscle in my body is screaming. The darkness is gone, and with it, the numbness.

"What's wrong?"

"Remember when we were talking about how the demon side of me helps me to ignore my wounds?"

"Yeah."

"That's side's gone now, and all that pain came rushing back all at once. It hurts."

"There's no way you can fight a Rougarou like this." Dan sighs and rubs my back in a soothing motion. "Maybe we should call Silas."

"He can't heal this. He already tried."

He says something so low I can't hear it. I'm betting I don't want to either.

"I'm hoping Zeke can find me more of that potion he gave me for Eli's funeral."

"I don't think that'll help either. What if the curse inside you feeds on it?"

"Why would it feed on a potion?"

He purses his lips. "Your dad didn't tell you, but it was black magic he used to make that."

Another mental slap in the face. Zeke knows how I feel about black magic.

"Don't get mad at him. He was doing what he had to do to get you through. If you hadn't been able to go to Eli's funeral, it would have devastated you. That was the only way to get you there."

"Sometimes we do things we don't want to do to protect the people we love."

Our mothers are prime examples. Mine tried to kill me as the only means she had to keep me safe. Dan's mother murdered his birth mother to keep him safe. People do horrible things to protect the ones they love.

"I'm not sure how to protect you from this curse. The only potion I know strong enough to subdue your pain is black magic, which will feed the curse growing inside you. Don't think I haven't heard your stomach growling."

I smile in between winces. Moving back to the seat is going to hurt.

"Black magic can't protect me, Dan. It's not something someone like me should ever use. It will only feed the darkness inside of me." I take a deep breath and tell him about my fears, about how this all started when I took in the wraiths. I should have told him a long time ago, but I was afraid. Afraid it would push him away, but I should have known better.

"Please don't hide things from me anymore, Mattie. Please."

Another sharp pain rips into my

shoulder when I try to sit up to look at him, and I whimper.

Dan does something I never expected he'd do in a million years. He calls out for my mother.

Not Georgina, but my mother.

Rhea.

I glare at him.

"You said it yourself, black magic can't help you, but maybe white magic can."

"White magic?" Rhea's soft, musical voice fills the car. We turn to see her sitting in the car seat. She's dressed in the same white robes I saw her in before, her hair piled on top of her head, curls cascading around her face. She's beautiful.

"You can leave. Dan shouldn't have called for you."

She smiles. "You look like you can use some help."

"I don't need your help."

"You're cursed with magic you can't combat because of the demon half that lives in you. Even if you somehow manage to kill the beast, it's not going to make all that darkness recede, my Rose. It's feeding off it, growing stronger every minute. Do you really want that?"

I don't, but I don't want her help either. I don't want to owe her.

"Can you help her?" Dan asks. "Can you heal her?"

"I can."

Well, dang.

"Please, Mattie, let her help you."

"I…"

Dan kisses me to shut me up. "Let her do this for you so you can save Cass and maybe others. You know that thing is out there, feeding, killing. You can't save anyone if you don't get some help."

"Why do you always have to be the voice of reason?"

"Because he's your light in the night," Rhea says. "He's your lighthouse in a sea of darkness, the same as you are for all the ghosts that come to you. He's the reason you exist, and you're the reason he exists."

As much as I dislike the woman for abandoning me to a fate worse than death, I have to admit that was the nicest thing anyone's ever said to me about Dan. It sums him up perfectly.

"Let her help you, Squirt. For me?"

Why does he have to use that tactic? He knows I'll give in.

"Fine, but I want it known, I am against this."

Rhea laughs. "You are as stubborn as your father."

I like to think so.

She holds out her hand, and I tentatively put mine in hers. Her fingers are warm, so warm I shiver. I'm inherently cold, and when a heat source gets near, my body reacts. It reaches out greedily for as much heat as it can suck up. That's what Rhea is. She's made up of energy and who knows what else, but she generates more heat than anyone I know, including Eli, whose body became what I needed—a furnace.

"This is dark magic," she says after a minute. "What happened?"

"Rougarou," Dan tells her when I stay quiet. "She and her friend Cass were attacked. Think you can heal him too?"

"Of course," Rhea murmurs and closes

her eyes.

Heat crawls out of her hand and up my arm, spreading out like the strands of a spiderweb until I'm covered from head to toe in all that fire. It burns as it cleanses my body of the curse infecting me. I can feel it wrap around the darkness in my soul, scouring it out of all the cracks and filling those cracks with light. I see it as clearly as if I'm drawing it. She's putting more glue in my soul.

"Someone removed your soul." The anger in her voice is surprising.

"It was done to make a point. I wasn't taking care of it, and Silas thought if I could see what was wrong, I wouldn't put myself in situations where I consumed hundreds of wraiths."

"You did what?" She pauses in her healing to look up, startled and afraid. "Why would you do that?"

"I caused the mess, so I cleaned it up."

She shakes her head but doesn't say anything else until she's done. Even the pain in my shoulder is gone. I look down at my arms, and the wounds are gone. Everything is gone.

"There, you're all cleaned up again, better than new." She smiles, and I wish I could return it, but there's a lot of bitterness there. Maybe Dan's not the only one unable to find a way to forgive.

"Thank you."

While it doesn't sound very genuine, I said it. That counts, right?

Dan frowns, clearly not agreeing.

"Thank you, Rhea." The sincerity in his voice mocks my half-hearted tone. "I appreciate it more than I can tell you."

"She's my Rose. I'll always come when she needs me."

"I will call you later to help Cass?" Dan asks.

She nods.

"Thank you again."

Seeing I'm not going to say anything else, she disappears, leaving me alone with Dan.

"Mattie…"

"Don't Mattie me. She abandoned me to be sacrificed to Deleriel. It's going to take a long, long time before I get past that."

"She healed you completely."

"I said thank you."

He shakes his head and deposits me into the passenger seat and snaps my seatbelt into place. Handing me his phone, he starts the car. "Call Caleb. Tell him to call Cass and have him meet us at your dad's and to tell Eric to have his hacker friend come along as well. Let's get this finished before that thing kills anyone else."

At least he has a plan. One that doesn't involve him pushing me on the whole Rhea matter.

It's more than I have.

My father is waiting for us on the porch.

He's sitting in the rocking chair, a cup of sweet tea on the small table beside the chair. Beside his chair sits his shotgun.

Crap on toast. He's pissed.

I don't think he'd actually shoot Dan.

Considering who he is, he could probably get away with it, though.

"He's mad."

"That's the understatement of the year, Officer Dan."

He gives me a very unfriendly look, and I grin wolfishly. Time for my boyfriend to meet my father, the man everyone in the south is terrified of.

"You." Zeke doesn't stand, doesn't shout, just speaks quietly the minute we step out of the car. "Sit."

Dan glances at me. "What? He's not talking to me."

"Don't think you're getting off that easy, *ma petite*."

My eyes widen at the cold note in Zeke's voice. He's never spoken to me in that tone before. I don't like it. Not one bit. It brings back my earlier conversation with Dan. That fear I've buried rears its ugly head. What if I've gone too far and Zeke walks away?

Dan's fingers find mine and squeeze. "He loves you."

How does he always know what I'm thinking?

"What does that mean?" Zeke asks. "Of course, I love my daughter."

"Old insecurities," I mutter and walk with Dan up the porch steps, clutching his hand so tight I might have cut off the circulation. Zeke's been mad at me before, but he's never looked at me with so much ice in his eyes. It upsets me more than I want to admit. I love my dad as much as I do Dan.

Zeke frowns. "Insecurities?"

"She grew up in foster care," Dan reminds him. "When people got too fed up with her, they tossed her back into the system, and she got shipped around from home to home."

Understanding blooms across his expression. "Sweetheart, I would never toss you back. You're my daughter. I love you even when you do things that test my patience…" His voice trails off when he gets a look at me. "What…"

"I called in a favor," Dan finishes before Zeke can ask the question. "She's completely healed, the curse is gone, and even the metaphysical injuries she didn't tell us about have been taken care of."

I stomp his foot. He did not need to tell my dad that.

"What injuries?"

"If you promise to leave that shotgun where it is, I'll tell you."

"I haven't made up my mind about that yet." Zeke's stance widens into a fighter's pose. "You spent the night with my daughter holed up in some cheap motel doing…"

"Oh, for Pete's sake," I burst out. "I wasn't in any shape to do anything last night but sleep. I was in so much pain, I could barely move. Dan cares too much about my safety to even so much as try something when I'm hurt. You should know better, Papa."

His lips thin. He knows I'm right.

"Besides, I'm eighteen. I can do what I want."

His eyes narrow, the rage back. Part of me shrinks back from it because he might leave, but the old Mattie rears her head, the one who always went on the defensive and lashed out. My emotions have been running too high the last couple days.

"And you're still my daughter. I will not have you…"

"No." I put as much force into my words as I can. "You can't tell me what to do. I love you, Papa, but no one dictates to me what I will or won't do. Not you, not Dan, not Silas."

Well, maybe Silas, but I keep that to

myself. Silas would actually hurt me if he has to. Physically hurt me. I think I'd do just about anything to prevent that, having been on the receiving end of it before.

"She sounds just like you at that age." The fondness in my grandfather's words is unmistakable. "Come, give your *grand-père* a hug, girl."

Josiah Crane is every inch the grandfather with his salt and pepper hair and warm blue eyes. Zeke's eyes. He looks a lot like my father, and that sets me at ease around him. My grandmother, I'm always a little on edge around. She's just so proper. Josiah, however, is not at all proper. You can tell by the long cargo shorts he's wearing and his green t-shirt. If Lila saw him wearing this, she'd have a heart attack.

"Morning, Grandpa." I disentangle myself from Dan and hug the old guy. I'm still not as comfortable with him as I am Zeke, but we're working on it.

"It's well past noon, Emma. What time did you crawl out of bed?"

"Early." I wrinkle my nose in disgust.

Saturday mornings should be spent lazing under the blankets, trying to keep the sun out of your eyes while you luxuriate in the ability to sleep in.

His gaze sweeps over me, taking in every single detail. "Ezekiel said you were a bloody mess, but you look fine to me."

My own lips curl in disgust. "Talk to him." I jerk my thumb toward Dan. "This wasn't my idea."

Now, that got Zeke's attention. "What did he do?"

"I called Rhea." Dan folds his arms and leans against the wide white pillar. "Mattie was in a bad way. The darkness in her was feeding off the curse, and it started to affect her. She was flying off the handle and almost hurt her brother. And me."

"What?"

A sigh stumbles past my lips. "What he said."

"Explain." The clipped words drive me further away from my father. I don't like him being angry with me. It makes me nervous. It's times like this that I wonder if I will ever get past the insecurities of growing up in foster care, unwanted and shuffled from one home to another. Zeke loves me. I know that, but those old fears have taken root.

Dan spends the next few minutes telling them both everything, leaving out not one single detail. Including what I'd done to that woman in the voodoo shop and the deal I'd made with her.

"Silas seems to be a very bad influence," Zeke says after Dan's finished.

"No more so than anyone else." My eyes warn him about the ultimatum about to fly out of his mouth. I will not stop visiting Silas. He's my family. Yes, he's a demon who doesn't hesitate to do what's necessary, but he's saved me more times than I can count. It's why I trust him, or at least trust him as much as I can. He's been there for me, didn't abandon me. He's proven himself.

"Why didn't you tell us, poppet?" Josiah steps in before his son can put his foot in his mouth. "We would have helped you."

"I…" Clearing my throat, I wrap my arms around myself and turn so I can stare out at the wide, sweeping driveway.

"Emma Rose."

My father is right behind me. I don't want to turn and see the disappointment in his eyes.

"I was handling it."

"Clearly, you weren't."

I flinch. I knew he was going to be disappointed in me.

His hand lands on my shoulder, and I hunch in on myself. "I'm not saying that to be cruel, *ma petite*. It is simply a statement of fact. This world is new to you. Yes, you've seen ghosts all your life, but you've been shielded from the darker side of the paranormal world. Your own gifts were buried deep and almost killed you when they woke up. My point is that while you don't know how to handle what is going on inside you, we do. Papa and I are well equipped to guide you through everything you're feeling, help you learn to control it. That's what family does, *ma petite*. We're there for each other."

"But that's what's hard for me," I confess and rub my arms. Some of the heat Rhea infused in me when she healed me is leaving, and I'm starting to get cold again.

"What?" Zeke spins me around so he can look at me. A distressed sound is ripped from him, and he hauls me into a bear hug. I have no idea what my expression must look like, but it upset him.

"She's come a long way from the scared and snarky kid I met in a hospital, but deep down, she's still that scared little girl," Dan says softly. "She's still afraid to let herself love us, to let us love her. She's afraid we'll leave."

"Everyone always leaves me," I whisper against Zeke's shirt. "They get tired of me and all the trouble I cause. No one stays. No one but Dan."

"You're never getting rid of me, Squirt." I can hear the smile in his voice, and I know he's thinking of the ring he bought. I wonder what it looks like.

"Emma, I thought we settled all this last year." Zeke hugs me tighter. "There is nothing you can do or say that will ever make me 'get rid of you.' Don't you know that, *ma petite*? What has caused all this to come back up?"

"It was the Rougarou curse. It heightened every emotion she had, and I think it pulled out all those old vulnerabilities she hid so well." Dan pushes off the column and walks over to us. "It made her remember all those feelings she lived with for most of her life and amplified them. I think it's going to take a bit for them to settle back down. Rhea healed her physically and scoured out all the darkness in her soul, but only love and time can do away with her fears."

"That, I can do." Zeke kisses the top of my head. "Anything you need from me, it's yours, sweet girl. There is absolutely nothing I won't do for you."

"Does that mean you're not gonna shoot Dan with that shotgun?" I peek up at him, a half-smile gracing my lips. What he said helped to ease some of the insecurity rearing its ugly head, but Dan's right. That curse had done a number on me, and I didn't even realize it until now. I'm terrified of losing all the people who love me, the people I love. It would be just my luck, though. I always end up broken and bruised in some fashion or other.

"I don't know."

"What are you going to do when he moves down here?"

Zeke growls. "I…"

"I'm almost twenty years old, Papa."

"The girl's right." Josiah yawns. "She's a grown woman with her own life. If she wants to move in with the boy, you can't stop her. I guarantee if you do, she'll move in with him just to spite you."

"How do you know I'd do that?"

"Because it's what your father would have done at your age." Josiah winks. "Now, come on in the house, and we'll tell you what we learned from the swamp queen."

"The swamp queen?" I let Zeke lead me into the house, following along to the office. My favorite couch is waiting, and I make a beeline for it. "This couch is so coming with me when I finally get an apartment."

"You want to steal my nap couch?" Zeke looks horrified at the thought.

"Well, I'll only steal it if I have to. If you give it to me, then it means I won't have to make Dan help me break in and steal it."

Josiah snorts—yes, snorts. I'm learning to do it too. I haven't quite mastered it yet. "That boy is a police officer. It's not in him to break the law."

Dan and I share a smile. Josiah couldn't be more wrong. I'd talked Dan into breaking into a house before. We got into some hot water, but it's proof the boy will do anything for me.

"What's that sly smile about?" Josiah frowns.

"Nothing." I sink down into the cushions and sigh from sheer bliss. "I love this thing."

Dan takes a seat beside me, and I turn to snuggle into him. "You good?" he asks.

"No, but I'm better."

He kisses my forehead and leans back,

turning his full attention on my father. "What have you found out?"

"The woman in the swamp has no idea who cast that curse."

"Are you sure?" I ask. "Her place was heavily warded against it. Even Cass thinks she might know something."

"Trust me, *ma petite*, no one lies to me."

That's the God's truth. It's an ability I inherited too. If we ask a question with the force of our will behind it, there is no lying. Well, usually. Dan and I are protected against it, thanks to Silas. That protection almost cost Dan his life, and it's not something I like to think about. It hurt like nobody's business too.

"There are ways around that." Dan shifts and raises his arm so I can get closer. The need to have him wrapped around me is too strong to resist. It's all this stupid insecurity I'm feeling. I know he's here and that he's not leaving, but part of me is still afraid and needs reassurance.

Zeke cocks his head. "What do you mean?"

Dan arches a brow in reply. "I know enough about this world now to know there's a workaround for everything if you're willing to pay the price."

"Did you pay the price for such a protection?"

"No." The falsehood slides as easily off his tongue as it would mine. Hanging out with me has been such a bad influence on him. He never used to be able to lie, but it comes so easily to him now. And that causes me just a moment of pain. I don't want Dan to ever lose his goodness. He's that guy who would do anything for anyone. Being with me has hardened him, and I hope despite that, he never changes. He believes in truth, justice, and all that nonsense.

I couldn't care less about most of it.

"Trust me, even if she found a way to lie, by the end of our session, she wouldn't have."

Dan tenses. I can only guess at what Zeke did, and none of it legal. Dan hates that Zeke partakes in illegal activity, but he stays away from all that because of me.

"Is she still breathing?" he asks softly, his muscles ripcord tight.

"Of course. I would never upset the Loa that way."

"The who?" I have no clue what he's referring to.

"The spirits," Dan explains, his voice buttery soft. A sure sign he's pissed. "When doing voodoo, the Loa is called upon to grant the request of the spellcaster. They're sacred and can get rather testy if irritated or upset. You do not want to harm someone they protect."

"Like a voodoo queen or priestess?"

"Exactly like," Dan agrees with a nod. "Don't piss off the Loa."

"So, if she's not the one who cast the curse, why was her place so heavily warded against it?"

"Because the Loa told her to do it." Zeke takes a seat in the chair across from us after getting him and his father a drink. He didn't bother asking Dan if he wanted one. Dan has turned them down so many times, I think my father gave up on him drinking. Not that I care. I like that he doesn't drink so much. I've seen what drinking can do to people. It's not pretty.

"You know, for someone who didn't even believe in the supernatural, you sure do know about it." I snuggle closer, feeling my anxiety start to melt away. Dan always calms me. He's the best medicine for me right now.

"I've been reading from Heather's library. She has more books on the subject than anyone I know. When you decided to move down here, I wanted to get up to speed on some of the things that could hurt you. There's more than I like. It's part of the reason I stepped up my timeline on moving down. I can't protect you if I'm not here."

"I don't need you to protect me." It's great that he likes to do it, but sometimes a girl gets suffocated by all the men in her life trying to protect her.

The force of his sigh ruffles my hair. "Squirt, I get that you want to be you without any help from anyone, but sometimes it's good to have a little help even when I know you don't really need it."

"He's right, poppet." Josiah intervenes before I can respond. "We all know you're capable. You faced down a Rougarou and survived. We know you don't need our help, but we want to be here for you anyway. We want to help you because we love you, not because we don't think you're a strong, capable young woman."

"You should go into politics, Grandpa. You have a gift for words."

"Bite your tongue!" He makes a horrified face. "I hate politics."

And that's the God's truth. I've tried to pull him into a few conversations about current events, and he just laughs, saying that's for better minds than his to sort.

"Could she tell you anything about who might have cast the curse?" I ask, trying to steer us back on track. The sooner I get Dan out of here, the better. He's getting more and more pissed by the minute thinking of what Zeke may have done to get answers from the old hag.

"There are only a handful of people powerful enough to cast that curse. She gave me a few names. One died, and the other two I am presently looking for. I am more than sure I can find them before the end of the moon cycle. Not that you need that anymore, but I suppose the hunter does."

"No, Rhea said she would heal him too." We called everyone to meet here. I can't whisk Dan away until we get everything sorted. *Grrrr.* "Everyone's on their way here, and Eric is bringing his friend who can hack into the NOPD databases."

"Why would you need to hack into those?"

"I had a vision last night about the roogie. I drew what he looks like, but without being able to access the DMV or police databases, we have no way to identify the guy."

"I didn't know you were still having visions."

I shrug. "It's the whole shaman bloodline. I can't stop the visions like I could everything else. This is the first one I've had since…since Charlotte."

I started to say since the ones about Eli's curse, but I don't like to think about that. The less I think about Eli, the less I hurt.

"Anyway, do you have a secure internet connection Jordan can use? One that won't lead straight back here?"

Dan makes a noise. He's not happy about this, but it's not like he has a better idea.

Zeke smirks. He knows how much our illegal activity bothers Dan. He likes to irritate my boyfriend, I think, just because he is my boyfriend. Zeke doesn't want to see me as a grown woman but wants to keep me as the little girl he remembers. I haven't been an innocent little girl since before I could talk. Having a heroin junkie for a mother forced me to grow up super-fast. I took care of her more than she did me some days.

"Of course, but you won't need a hacker. I have my own login credentials you can use."

Dan and I both sort of look at him with shocked expressions on our faces. How the heck would he get credentials to log into a police database?

"Don't ask, and I won't be forced to lie." Zeke smiles.

Before we can respond to that little bit of information, the doorbell rings.

He's literally saved by the bell.

Nathaniel is still just as uncomfortable in my father's house as he was the first time I brought him here. Not that I blame him. Zeke is not overly friendly. He's not rude, per se, just not friendly. You can tell he doesn't want him here, but he's not going to let all those good manners of his fail him now. His mother would beat him. Lila Crane is not someone to cross.

Mary and Caleb are at least on speaking terms. Not sure if they agreed to sit down and talk, but I hope so.

Jordan arrived a few minutes after everyone else and is presently sitting at Zeke's desk, with Zeke hovering right behind him, working with the sketch I gave him. It was easy enough to scan into the computer, and then he started with the DMV. I didn't really pay any attention after I handed it over to him, content to snuggle against Dan. All those feelings the curse brought back up are still very present. He was right about time and love making them go away again.

"You okay?" I ask him.

"No." He's staring holes into Zeke and Jordan. The kid has an unruly head of red hair, making him stand out against the very elegant backdrop of the old plantation manor house.

"I'm sorry." That little worm of doubt niggles its way back into my thoughts.

"For what?"

"For putting you in a situation like this, one where you're forced to ignore your morals, to ignore your instincts."

His arms tighten around me. "It's not your fault, Squirt. We don't have legal means at our disposal. I'm not a cop anymore."

"But you will be."

He nods. "I miss it, but I don't miss the

stares and the whispers and the snide jokes behind my back."

"Because of your mom?"

"Yeah. I couldn't do my job effectively anymore. I was ready to bash some heads near the end, there."

"*You,* lose your cool?"

"Even I have a breaking point. I can only hear my mother talked about so much."

It's one of the reasons I keep my feelings about Ann Richards to myself. He loves her, and he doesn't need me telling him I despise the woman. When he was lying in that hospital bed dying, she didn't even fight for him. It was like she was glad he was dying, telling him to move on. If Caleb hadn't been there, I think I might have really hurt her. He grabbed me when I lunged at her. Mrs. Richards and I haven't spoken since that day.

I don't know if Dan knows about that or if he saw it from his vantage point as a wandering spirt. It's not something we talk about. I want to think it was his mother's way of protecting him from everything, but I can't. I think she did it out of spite. To me, to the Malones. She didn't want him to have anything to do with us, and him dying made sure she got what she wanted. Maybe it's the cynic in me, but that's what I firmly believe. She loves Dan, yes, but I think her own agenda comes first sometimes.

I am not looking forward to seeing her when we go back for the trial.

"Got it!" Jordan calls out, excited.

We all rush over to the desk, pretty much forcing my father to move back or risk being trampled.

"His name is Hershal Montgomery. Lives at 1311 Bayou Road."

Cass and I share a look. Seems appropriate, seeing as how we were attacked in the bayou. He'd arrived soon after Jordan with his cousin Robert. They gave him crutches when they sent him home late last night, but he couldn't drive with a broken leg, so Robert was his chauffeur. Both of them had been surprised I wasn't covered in bruises and cuts but hadn't said anything.

In fact, they'd all been shocked, but no

one mentioned it. I guess they thought Zeke did something to fix me.

"Can you log me into the police database?" Dan shoos Jordan out of the chair and directs his question to Zeke, who does as asked. Once he's in, Dan takes back over. "I'm running a search to see if there've been any reports at that address."

"His family," I murmur.

Dan nods. "We need to know as much as we can."

Seconds after he types in his search parameters, a report comes up. They had indeed found his family, but not him. There was a flyer circulating with all Mr. Montgomery's details. The report is a little over two weeks old.

"There shouldn't be a police presence there anymore." I straighten. "You up for a little B-and-E, Officer Dan?"

He scrubs a hand over his face. "As long as there's no more snakes."

"Snakes?" Nathaniel and Zeke ask at the same time.

Dan grins but shakes his head. "Forget it."

"Come on, let's go be deviants." I link my arm in his and look at everyone else. "Caleb, you, Mary, Eric, and Jordan head to the local library and find out as much information as you can on the murders and any reports of missing people or animal attacks over the last three weeks. Nathaniel, you're coming with me and Dan. Papa, can you work on trying to find the other two voodoo people?"

My father's eyebrows raise so high they might jump off his face, but my grandfather laughs. "She's just like you, boy. Girl knows how to get people moving."

A small smile breaks through, and my father nods. "Sure you don't want to take over the business?"

"Nope, not even a little bit. There is something else I want to do, though, and I hope you can help me with it. We'll talk about that after we deal with the roogie."

"Rougarou," Cass corrects me. "Wha' do you want me and Rob to do?"

"I have something special for you guys."

"Well?" Cass prompts when I don't go

into further detail.

"Caleb, you guys get going. Cass, you follow us. Robert, don't let my father murder my brother while we're gone."

Robert laughs, but neither my father nor my brother does. I'm serious. Robert may not think so, but they know I am.

Dan helps Cass up the stairs to my bedroom. Once we're inside and the door is locked, I call for Rhea. She appears instantly, a smile on her face.

"Hello, my Rose."

She always calls me Rose. Papa told me it's what she called me since before I was born. She knew I was a girl.

"This is Cass. You said you could help him as well."

She turns her attention to him and walks over. "He is cursed, but it is not as severe as yours was."

"He's not part demon either."

She cocks her head, thinking. "Yes, that would explain why it spread so fast through you. It fed on the demon half of your soul."

Cass's eyes shoot to me. "You were worse?"

I grimace, thinking of what I'd done. "Yes. I almost hurt both my brother and Dan. I did hurt the voodoo lady."

"Emma..." His voice trails off. He sounds upset, but I don't think it's *at* me, but *for* me.

I toss him my brightest smile. "I'm all good now. This is Rhea. She's going to remove the curse from you."

He frowns. "How is dat possible?"

"She's gifted like that."

He turns all his attention to Rhea and really looks at her for the first time. She's still wearing that white toga that looks like something one of the Greek Goddesses would have worn. It's a dead giveaway. She needs to wear some normal clothes.

"Who are you?" He leans away from her when she reaches out to place her hand on his head.

"She's someone who can help you, so sit still. It doesn't hurt."

"Rose is right, child. This won't hurt." She places her hand on his forehead, and he gasps. It's all that warmth spilling through him, healing everything, even the broken leg. When my mother is done, she steps back and gives him a brilliant smile. "There, you see?"

He blinks several times, his gaze bouncing from his leg, to Rhea, to me. "I...t'ank you."

"You are most welcome." She turns back to me. "You will be seeking out the cursed?"

"That's the plan."

"You are meant to do this work. I had hoped you would take another path, but since you insist on danger, will you let me put a protection upon you?"

"What kind of protection?"

"Your body is very much human and more fragile than most hybrids. You gained none of your grandfather's resistance to injury, or mine. I can at least help you with that. Make it harder to hurt you."

"Will it stop the damage to my brain?"

"I healed that as well this morning, but as more and more of your abilities wake up, your mind and body will struggle. Your human self is not able to handle all that you are. Your brain will continue to be harmed."

"But you can stop that?"

She nods with a gentle smile. "You are my child. I wish no harm to come to you. I saw this morning just how fragile you are, and it has worn on my heart since. You got my heart, but not my ability to heal myself."

"Heal yourself?" An old conversation I had with Silas comes back. It was after Mrs. Olsen had smashed my hands and I'd fought Jonas, the soul sucker. I'd used what I now know to be soul fire, and it had partially healed my hands. Silas finished it for me. "Silas said I could do that, but I just hadn't learned how yet."

"The demon told you this?" She approaches me and holds out her hand. "May I?"

Dan gives me a nudge, and I hesitantly place my hand in hers. That same warmth suffuses me, but I can feel her searching, her mental hand ruffling around in my mind. She hits a door, one locked so tight it bounces her back, and she staggers away from me.

"Oh, my." She rights herself. "I was

wrong. You do have the means to protect yourself, it's just locked away. Someone did this on purpose. I can feel the residual magic emanating from it."

Cass sucks in a breath, but I don't look at him. I keep my focus on Rhea. Someone messed with my mind?

"Has your father…"

"No, Papa wouldn't do that. He'd be the first one trying to break down the door."

She frowns. "Your father…"

"Is not who you think he is. I know what they told you, that he was a bad man who wanted to hurt me. It was Georgina who wanted to hurt me, not Papa."

"I have spent all these years believing Amanda would keep you safe from him, and you suffered because of my actions."

"My mama loved me. She did what she did to protect me."

"I know." She gives me a sad smile. "Someone locked these abilities away, though."

"What abilities?"

"Healing, for one. Your demon blood

should make your human body almost immune to injuries, but yet it's very human. My blood should make you invincible, for the most part, or at the very least so hard to hurt, a gunshot would be like a paper cut. Yet you're vulnerable."

She looks upset, and now I'm curious.

"Maybe it's good that all that's locked away." Kane's warning comes to mind. "There are those who don't want me any stronger than I am."

"I do not understand. You sound as if you are afraid, Rose."

Oh, yeah. I'm terrified. "Do you know who Kane is?"

She nods. "He is your…trainer?"

"Yes. It's his job to teach me how to be a reaper. He gave me a warning."

"He threatened you?" Ice replaces the concern in her eyes, and I shrink back against Dan. The woman is freaking scary when she gets mad. I can feel her anger rolling out from her in waves. Even Dan flinches.

"No, he warned me. His bosses, they're all in agreement that I shouldn't exist. I'm not tied to the strings of destiny anymore because Dan isn't. Our souls are linked. They were going to smite me once I killed Deleriel, but then my soul shattered, and you bound everything but my reaping abilities. He told me a bit ago, they're watching me again. If I get too strong, I'm afraid they might do something."

"No one will touch you." Her expression turns fierce. "Smite my daughter? I'll smite them all."

"Wait, I don't think that's a good idea." I reach out to grab her arm because she looks like she's ready to go do just that. "Smiting them only causes problems. They keep the balance between life and death, the schedule of death on time. Hurting them only hurts millions of other people."

"Hurting you is unacceptable."

"I'm not ready to give up and let them hurt me. I'm being cautious. If I die, Dan dies, and there's not a force in this world that could get away with that. I'd come back in death to avenge him."

His arms tighten around me, and I lay

my hand on top of his where they're linked around my stomach. He's afraid I'm going to wig out again. I'm good for the minute. The assurances earlier helped.

"This door, can you open it?"

She shakes her head. "It's something I've never come up against. I must think on how to do it. Someone as strong or stronger than I am did this, I just do not know who. There are not many of us left, or at least active. My brothers and sisters have all fallen into a deep sleep. Once their followers abandoned them, their will did as well."

Cass's eyes are about to bug out of his head, and I suppress a laugh. Poor guy. This is not what he expected when he asked me what I was.

"Maybe Mama had someone do it when she was trying to find ways to protect me against everything?"

"No. I've spoken with Amanda at length. This is something that was done to you, to make you vulnerable. Someone meant you harm."

Well, fudgepops.

"Someone worse than a Fallen Angel?"

Dan asks, his arms going rigid.

"Far worse. A god did this to her. I do not know why, but I intend to find out."

"You said you could do something to help her now, though? To keep her from getting herself killed?" Dan takes several deep breaths, trying to get control of his fear. He's afraid, but so am I. A Fallen Angel is one thing, but a god? I don't think even I can take on one of those and survive.

"Yes, of course, but she must allow me to do it."

"What exactly are you going to do?"

She frowns, searching for the right words. "It is like a coat of paint, but one that hardens your shell to injury. It's not visible, but it gives you far more protection than even those sigils on your back."

Silas would gut her for even saying such a thing.

"But the headaches won't come back?"

"I can't promise they'll stay away forever, but when they do, I can heal them. You'll be stronger, faster, and your instincts will run on a higher alert level so you're always more aware."

"And Dan?"

She smiles. "You love this young man?"

"Yes."

"I can see the tether that ties you both together. It's as strong as a steel cable."

I'm not surprised.

"The physical protection only applies to you, and it's something I can give *only to you* because you are my child. You are a part of me, and it's a part of myself I am giving you. It would not work on your young man."

I don't know if I want any part of her. She abandoned me to Deleriel.

"It doesn't matter if it can't be extended to me." Dan drops his head on top of mine. "I only die if she does. If this protection can keep her from dying, then it keeps me safe as well."

And he had to point that out, didn't he? He knows I won't say no if it means keeping him safe.

"Fine."

"I love you," he whispers.

I scrunch up my nose. He knows I'm

pissed.

"This will hurt."

Freaking awesome. I step out of Dan's arms and try to mentally prepare myself for the pain. I do my best not to put myself in situations that will cause me pain, but there's no helping this one.

Her palm goes flush against my forehead, but there's no heat this time, no delicious warmth. Only pain. So much pain. My legs buckle beneath me as fire scorches over me, invades my bloodstream, travels through all the way to my heart, my brain, burning away everything and leaving a charred path in its wake.

The sounds coming out of my mouth are unrecognizable, even to me. Somewhere in the middle of it all, I hear heavy pounding on the door. Zeke, maybe, but I hurt too much to even care.

And then it's done.

I fall over and curl into a ball, my body shaking so hard I'm afraid it won't stop. The door is kicked open, and Zeke and Nathaniel both burst in the same time Dan picks me up off the floor. The shaking won't stop.

"What happened?" Zeke demands, his eyes on me.

I try to speak, but the only thing that comes out is the sound of my chattering teeth.

"She'll be safe now." Rhea comes to stand by me. "I am so sorry you had to endure that, but it was necessary."

"Who are you?" Zeke snarls and strides over, ready to do her bodily harm.

"Hello, Ezekiel." Rhea smiles softly, the musical lilt in her voice sadder than I've ever heard it.

"This is Rhea," Dan tells him, but he doesn't need to add the part about her being my mother. He knows.

He's frozen, shock as clear as day on his face.

"Did you hurt her?" Nathaniel isn't frozen and is moving with a grace of a cat but the deadly intent of a tiger.

"Only as much as was necessary." She turns back to me and rests her palm against my face. The heat is back, and it drives away the cold. My shaking subsides. "Better?"

I nod, and Dan is the only one with enough presence of mind to tell her thank you, which she brushes off. "Call me if I am needed." And then she's gone.

"Who was that?"

"An old friend," Dan tells my brother. "I called in a favor, and she healed both of them."

My gaze swivels to Cass, warning him not to say anything in front of Nathaniel. I'm not ready to tell him about Rhea yet. I may never be ready. He nods slightly.

"Did she hurt you?" Zeke asks, snapping out of his shock coma.

"Yes, but I told her to."

"You did what?"

"She granted Mattie her protection, made her harder to hurt. The process was extremely painful," Dan explains before Zeke has a stroke.

"I need OJ, and then we have to get going. We don't have a lot of time."

The pain is gone, but I'm still shaky. Sugar. I need sugar.

"Maybe we should wait a while…"

I shake my head. "No. The longer we wait, the more time he has to kill innocent people. I'm okay. I promise."

He doesn't look like he believes me, but he stops arguing.

Sugar and then some B-and-E.

What more could a girl ask for?

The street we're on feels a little worn-down, like it's seen better days even though the houses are well cared for and the yards tended. Maybe it's because of the death all around me. Dan and Nathaniel are oblivious to it, but I'm not. So many have lost their lives in this city from natural disasters like hurricanes, to old age, to murder. Those ghosts roam the city, and for those sensitive to them, we feel the gloom and the coldness. The constant state of gray. This street is one of the worst I've been on.

"It says we're here," Dan grouches and looks along the sides of the street for a sign. "I don't see it…"

"There." I point down a little side road. "Right there off Mitro." I let out a groan when he goes right by it and onto Esplanade Avenue. "You missed it."

"Yeah, I see that," he grumbles. He hates when I backseat drive, but then he shouldn't ignore me when I try to show him the right road. All men are stupid when it comes to directions. They won't stop and ask. Instead, they insist they know where they are even when they're hopelessly lost. Dan is not immune to this stupidity either.

Nathaniel sighs loudly in the back. I shake my head at him. He wanted to drive, saying he knew the city better than we did, but of course Dan refused. No man likes to release control of his vehicle. Even a rental. It's another stupid guy thing.

"Right there." I point again once he's turned around and headed in the right direction. "The homes are a little nicer up that way too. See the fancy fences?"

Nicer homes do not mean the place feels any less worn, though. The sense of despair engulfs me as soon as we turn onto Bayou Road. It might be the recent murders that have stained it. I'm not sure. But it's pressing in on me, almost suffocating me.

"Only half the street is nicer," Nathaniel drawls. "The other side has falling-down fences."

"I know, but I wasn't going to harp on the misfortune of people when they lost so much the last few years."

He leans back, tapping his fingers against the seat. "Truths are truths, whether or not we want to admit it or speak of it."

I get the feeling he's talking about more than just the homes on this street. He's been quiet since we left Zeke's. He saw Rhea. He has to have some idea of what she was. I once asked him what he would do if I had gifts that were godlike. It was a slip of the tongue, but Nathaniel is a watcher. He takes everything in and never forgets. At least that's my take on my brother. He has to be thinking back to that conversation.

If it were me, I'd be obsessing over it.

And if he figures it out, my biggest fear is that the power he can get from me will trump any familial loyalty that may be growing between us. He'll kill me to get those gifts.

"Does silver hurt this thing like it does a werewolf?"

"Don't you mean does silver actually hurt a werewolf?" Dan smirks.

Do I mean that?

"Well?" I ask when he doesn't say anything else. "Do silver bullets kill a werewolf, Mr. Research Guru?"

"You watch too many movies, Squirt."

"It doesn't?" I am truly shocked. All the horror movies agree on this. You can't change the rules this late in the game.

Nathaniel snickers in the back, and I frown at him. This is not funny. I thought I'd be safe it I had a silver bullet.

"It does, but it doesn't have to be just a bullet," Dan clarifies. "It can be any weapon made of silver. It's something about the purity of the metal."

"It's more biblical than that." Nathaniel leans forward. "Isn't that the house?"

My head snaps around, and true enough, he's right. It's wedged between two very large homes. The house, while not as big as the others around it, is just as nice as the other homes on this side of the street. Homes in this area are very Greek revival style, and the only reason I know this is because I've gotten into sketching some of the unique architecture that can be found in New Orleans. I'd even thought about changing my major to architecture. I still might. Psychology is cool, but I'd love to be able to put my love for art into something that can make money.

The house is all white with a dark gray trim, the door a bright blue for a pop of color. It screams nice and comfy, a perfect place to start a family. Which is probably what brought the Montgomerys here. The front yard is well maintained, and I know there's a deck out back with a child's swing set tucked up near the privacy fence.

Neighbors are out and about as we drive down the street. So much for me thinking this would be easy.

"Drive around to the next street and park. We need to go in the back way. The privacy fence should help to keep us hidden."

"You don't think the neighbors are going to call the cops when they see three strangers scaling the back fence?" Dan turns the car then parks in the first available spot he sees.

I grin. "Officer Dan, you doubt me?"

He shakes his head and laughs. He thought for sure we'd have gotten caught the last time I picked a lock and broke into a house. Well, we were, but only because of that frickin' pet boa constrictor that decided I was lunch. Ollie the snake. It is one of my more memorable trips into the criminal world.

We get out and start walking toward the back of the houses. This street isn't nearly as busy, so we're able to duck between two houses and slide around to the privacy fence. Nathaniel serves as a lookout, and Dan helps lift me up so I can grab the top of the six-foot fence and pull myself over. An *umph* escapes as I land on my butt on the other side.

"You good?" Dan peeks over the fence to where I'm lying.

"Aside from cracking my tailbone, I'll be fine."

He gets this pious look, and I know he's thinking it's what I get for breaking the law. I stick my tongue out at him, and he grins in return. He so knows he's busted.

Once they're both over the fence, Nathaniel reaches down and hauls me up. "Did you hurt yourself when you fell?"

"Nah, I'm good."

We're careful to stick to the shadows of the yard as we make our way to the back porch. I dig my lockpicking tools out of my pocket and set to work.

"You just keep those handy, do you?" Nathaniel asks, his gaze sweeping the yard.

"I grabbed them before we left Zeke's." Two more twists, and I've got it.

"Where did you learn to pick a lock?" Nathaniel's impressed. "Even I can't do it that fast."

"Foster care. When you get hungry

enough, you learn to get past locks."

He rears back like I've just punched him right in the face. Dan knows this already, though he hates when I talk about that time of my life. I used to steal to eat, and sometimes I even had to pick the locks on the pantry and the refrigerator in some of my foster homes. Nathaniel knows very little about my time in the system, and it can be a shock.

"You grew up hungry?" I can't even define the emotion in his words, but it's telling.

"I'm not anymore." I open the door and peek inside. We all put on gloves back in the car. I didn't want fingerprints left behind. I'd even braided my hair and pinned it up in a Princess Leia style. I look about twelve.

"If I had known…"

"But you didn't, and we can't change the past. We can only learn from it and move forward." I push the door open and walk inside. "Now, we need to look for anything that might tell us where Mr. Montgomery could be hiding out. There has to be a clue in this house somewhere."

"Sure you don't want to apply to the academy?" Dan whispers as he passes by.

"Bite your tongue."

He laughs and moves off deeper into the house.

"Emma." Nathaniel stops me, his eyes a mess of pain and regret. "I am so sorry. I didn't know. No one should ever be hungry."

"I'm okay, Nathaniel, really."

"I just have this urge to do something, to make it right." He looks so puzzled.

"I'm guessing this is a new emotion for you?"

He nods, unsure of himself. "I've never really cared about anything before. I love my grandparents, of course, but they taught me to put myself first and screw everyone else. I thought that was the right way, and then I met you. I see you with your family, with your father, and I realize maybe the way I was raised isn't the best way to be."

"Believe it or not, that's exactly what it was like growing up in foster care. No one's going to look out for you but you, so you put up walls, you keep people at arm's length. You never let yourself love anyone, and you don't think you're worth anyone's love. I was a cold, callous person who never cared about anyone or anything until I met Dan. He taught me how to love and how to be loved. If it weren't for him, I'd be an emotionless vacuum. It's okay to be scared of new emotions, but the most important thing to remember is that it's okay to change too."

"Change is hard."

"You're telling me. Change is the one thing that scares me more than anything else. I hate it, and I can go off the deep end when I'm forced to accept it. But it can be good, so don't fight it so hard."

"I promise you will never go hungry again as long as I have a breath left in my body. I won't allow it."

And this is why I ignore the uneasy feeling in my gut about Nathaniel. He's trying, and I can see him changing. I hear it in his voice. I just hope our relationship can survive his greed for power when he figures out what I am.

"Good to know. Now, why don't you

go into the living room and start looking over family albums."

"Family albums?"

I nod. "We want to figure out where he's hiding. It'll be someplace he knows well and feels safe. Most likely a vacation spot or something similar. There will be pictures of it, lots and lots of pictures. That's what I want you to look for. Dan went to check the office."

"Where are you going?"

"Upstairs."

He's still for a heartbeat. "Are you sure that's wise, given what's happened here and what you can do?"

"No, it's not wise, but it is the easiest way to get the information we need."

I just hope these spirits aren't murderous.

The first thing I noticed about the house when we came inside was how quiet it was, an unnatural stillness to everything neither Dan nor Nathaniel picked up on. The place was cold too. The AC wasn't running. The police or whoever came to close up the house must have cut it off.

There's also a stench. It smells of rot and decay. And something else. What, I'm not sure of, though. Taking a deep breath to help settle my nerves, I go upstairs, following the path Mr. Montgomery walked the day he found his family.

The upstairs is dark, so I flip on the hallway light, and my eyes zero in on the stained carpet. Bloody footprints track up and down it. The baby's room is at the end of the hall, and I know I should go in there first, but I can't make my feet move. I remember what had been left of little Davey, and I don't want to see that again.

The daughter's room isn't any better, though. The memory of her blank, empty eyes has been in the back of my mind since I woke up. It's something that will haunt me for years to come.

Children's ghosts are the worst, and unfortunately are the ones that seem most drawn to me. Maybe I'll check out the master bedroom and give my nerves time to decide they're strong enough to handle seeing the children again.

The master is nice, a big room with a king size bed and a TV on the wall. The whole room is done in soothing tones of soft, earthy green and browns, with a pop of red here and there, something I would have liked in any other situation. I look around, wondering what this family was like on their good days. Happy. That would be my best guess. That was the feeling I got from the father when I was in his memory. He loved his family.

The dresser holds a jewelry box that is open, flashes of silver and gold sparkling in the sunlight pouring in the room from the window directly across. A hairbrush sits beside it, waiting to be picked up. A vase with wilted flowers adorns the table beside the bed, which is unmade. They must not have had a cleaning crew come in yet. Then again, the house still belongs to Mr. Montgomery, so it might be they can't call in a crew.

Which would explain the godawful smell.

But it's cold.

The smell would get worse in the heat, but not the cold. With the ghosts here, the place has become a freezer, especially up here. I lean down and pick up the shirt that's been left lying in the floor. Folding it, I put it on the bed. It feels wrong to leave it on the floor.

The master bath is dark, but again, I flip the light switch. The towel Mr.

Montgomery put down so he wouldn't get the rug wet is still there. His razor is on the sink countertop amidst all his wife's lotions and makeup. Her brush is in the other room. It's a bathroom where lives were mixed and shared.

The whole place gives me such an intense feeling of sadness.

What happened here wasn't right and wasn't fair. No one deserved what happened to this man and his family. I'll find the person responsible for this if it is the last thing I do.

Flipping the light back off, I go back into the bedroom.

And sitting there on the bed is the little girl. She's wearing her Ariel princess nightgown, but it's hardly recognizable between the dried brown stains and the way it's torn up. Her skin has been ripped to shreds, gashes and chunks of flesh missing from almost every inch of her. One white sock remains on her foot, a few drops of blood marring the color.

I barely stop the scream from tearing out of my throat. I came up here looking for them. I wanted to find them.

Doesn't make this easier, though.

"Hello." I try for a smile, but I don't know if I quite manage it.

She cocks her head and stares at me curiously.

"You can see me?"

I nod and inch a little closer.

"Yes, I can."

"Nobody else can see me, not even Mommy"

Her mother couldn't see her? That's strange. Usually ghosts can see each other, especially if they are haunting the same place.

"Why can't Mommy see you?"

She looks down, her hand playing with the edges of her nightgown. A bone is all that's left of her index finger. The flesh and muscle have been ripped away.

"I was bad."

"How were you bad?"

"Mommy said not to open the door, not for anybody but her."

"And you did?"

She nods, keeping her head down. "It was Daddy," she whispers. "I wasn't afraid of Daddy."

My heart breaks. As scared as I was a minute ago, sadness replaces it.

"But it wasn't Daddy. He looked like my daddy, but it wasn't him."

"I know," I say softly, understanding why her mother can't see her. The child is hiding because she's afraid of what her mother will say. "It wasn't really your daddy. The bad man tricked you, so it wasn't your fault you opened the door."

"It wasn't?"

"No, baby, it wasn't. Mommy's not mad at you." I hope that is the case, anyway. You can never really tell with ghosts, but I'm making a judgement call. This family loved each other. I'm guessing that won't change in death.

A baby's cry echoes around us, and I flinch. It's loud in the stark quiet of the house. Scraping noises reach us, and I back up, not knowing what it is.

"Is that your mommy?"

She shakes her head, scooting off the bed and running toward me. My entire body clenches when she grabs me. The cold is so deep it goes right down into my bones, burning away all sensation except pain.

"What is it?"

"Not Daddy."

At first, I don't understand. I know it's not her daddy. We came here looking to find a clue as to where he might be.

A lightbulb goes off when she buries her head in my stomach. Not Daddy.

Oh, my God. Not Daddy.

I back up slowly and go into the bathroom, closing the door softly and turning the lock. I keep going until the back of my legs hit the toilet. The scraping sound, I know what it is. Its nails tearing along the walls.

We came looking for a clue to where Mr. Montgomery might be, and we ended up finding the man himself. He's been hiding in plain sight. Carefully, I pull out my phone and text Dan to warn him. This thing couldn't have found him or Nathaniel yet. I'd have heard the screams.

The baby's crying gets louder, and now it's joined by a woman screaming. The little girl holds on even tighter, her sobs severe. "Shhh, it's okay. We're okay."

"No…" she wails. "He's going to get us."

The bathroom doorknob jiggles, and I bite down on my fist to keep from screaming. This thing knows me; it knows my scent. That's why it's up here, why it's at the door.

The baby's cry. It was in the baby's room. It came from the baby's room when it smelled me.

I don't have anything in here to protect myself with. The only thing that even looks like a weapon is the curling iron. I reach over and plug it in, staying as quiet as I can. Not sure it won't just bust down the door, but I'm hopeful I can get the iron hot enough to at least hurt it. If I can cause it pain, I can run.

A low, deadly growl comes through the door. It knows I'm in here. The door vibrates with the force of that thing pushing against it. One good slam, and it'll be inside.

I stand up, dragging the kid with me. She won't let go. I'm battling my own fear, the burn from the iciness that is all ghost, and my worry about Dan and Nathaniel. They'll be up here any minute, and that thing will go after them.

My phone chirps with a text from Dan. He's coming up and will draw it away so I can get out.

As great as that plan sounds, it's not really so great. It puts Dan in danger, and I've faced off against this thing. This beast is deadly.

About the same time I pick up the curling iron, the roogie rams the door, and it bursts open. The little girl screams, and I lash out blindly with the curling iron. Not sure how hot it is, but it has to do.

The creature howls in pain, and I smash the iron into his face, ignoring the crunch of bone. When it staggers back, I run, the little girl holding on for dear life.

I make it three steps before its claw-like hands curl around my shoulder and yank me back. Hot, putrid breath rolls over me, and I gag, but I keep hold of my fear. It slams me up against the wall, and I turn my face away. His elongated nose nuzzles along my neck, the spiky tongue licking up, tasting my fear.

"Can't leave you alone for a minute, can I?"

Dan's almost amused tone snaps me out of my momentary panic. He's standing in the doorway, his sword blazing in his hand. The thing lights up like a Christmas tree when he's holding it and there is something to be judged. The Sword of Truth, given to him by an Angel the night Meg died, has become a part of him. It's a burden he will bear until he's no longer strong enough to do it anymore.

He walks forward like he doesn't have a care in the word, but I see the intent in his eyes. The beast snarls, turning so it's almost shielding me. It crouches low, ready to spring, but Dan is ready for it. He makes a sweeping motion with the sword, and the creature lets out the most pitiful howl you've ever heard. Dan presses forward, driving it away from me and toward the opposite wall, herding it.

The sword presses against the skin of its neck, blood trickling down onto the blade. Dan's body bows with whatever the sword is showing him. When it's done, he whispers, "You have been judged."

And then he plunges the blade deep into the creature's chest cavity.

The roogie goes stiff, an earsplitting howl rising out of it and flooding the room. When he pulls the sword back, the creature falls, sprawling out on the carpet. I creep closer but don't touch Dan. I know he's not in a place where it would be wise. The sword has him all hopped up on judgy juice. God only knows what it would say about me.

It's not like in the movies, where when you kill the werewolf, it shifts back to human form. The thing that used to be Mr. Montgomery doesn't change. It stays the same, half dog, half man.

"What the…?" Nathaniel bursts into the room and stops, staring at the thing on the floor and Dan standing over it, his shoulders heaving as he takes in all the sword showed him. He has to bear the sins of the sinner until it's time for him to pass the sword on to the next person strong enough to shoulder that burden.

I still think to this day the Angel who gave it to him did it out of spite. They were all pissed that Dan and I chose each other over him dying, and it caused a ripple effect. People died. People like Meg. They knew how honorable Dan was, they knew he felt guilty about everything, and they used that to make him shoulder this awful burden, knowing he'd accept because he thought he deserved it.

He and I haven't talked about this, but I know Dan better than he knows himself. I know why he took that sword, and we're going to talk about it one day soon. I won't have him suffering because of misplaced guilt.

Not that I don't think he's a good fit for the sword. He has the discipline to wield it without letting the sword control him. That's what is needed to hold one of the swords, but at the same time, I won't let it hurt him. Even if I have to forcefully sever the tie between the sword and him, I'll keep him safe…mind, body, and soul.

"Is he okay?" Nathaniel whispers.

"Give him a minute." I look down to see the little girl still stuck to my side. She's crying, but it's muffled. "See, the bad daddy is gone now. You're safe."

She looks up, big blue eyes wide and tear filled. "He won't come back?"

"No, he won't come back. Why don't you go find your mommy and your little brother, and then I'll help you all go somewhere safe, okay?"

"She won't be mad?"

"No, I promise."

Without a word, she lets go and races out of the room, running right through Nathaniel. He shudders. "What…"

"The ghost of a little girl just dived through you looking for her mommy."

"I didn't see a ghost."

I smile, really smile, for the first time all day. "You're not a reaper, Nathaniel. You can't see every ghost like I can. You only see the ones strong enough to allow you to see them or so far gone, they're homicidal. That kind of juice and anyone, even the worst skeptic out there, will catch a glimpse of them."

Dan runs to bathroom, and I'm hot on

his heels. He barely makes the toilet before he's heaving. Like he did for me last night, I hold his head and rub his back, and he spews up all the vile things he took in when the sword judged Mr. Montgomery.

"Is this the first time you've used the sword?"

He shakes his head before laying it down on the toilet lid. I reach up and flush it so he doesn't smell the stink. As upset as I am about him using the sword and not telling me, right now he doesn't need me yelling. His emotions are too raw.

"Better?" I ask after he's spent a few minutes just lying there.

"No, but I will be." He gets up and goes to the sink to wash out his mouth. "Are you hurt?"

"No. I stabbed it a couple times with the curling iron, but it never so much as scratched me."

"You stabbed a monster with a curling iron?" Nathaniel asks, incredulous.

"Well, yeah. It's all I could find in here to use as a weapon. That thing gets hot as a poker sitting in a fire."

"My girl's quick on her feet, if nothing else." Dan attempts a smile, but it turns into more of a grimace.

I approach him as cautiously as I would a wild animal and hold my hands up to show him what I'm doing before slipping an arm around him. "This okay?"

"It's always okay." He drops his chin onto the top of my head. "Thank you."

"For what?"

"For understanding what happened back there and that I needed space."

"You might have been reading up on all things paranormal, but I read up on those swords and their effects. You're not the only one who knows how to research."

Nathaniel glances back toward the bedroom. "Now what do we do?"

"Well, I go find the mom and her kids and help them move on, and then we figure out what to do with that mess in there."

"I'll call Caleb. He'll know what to do." He lets me go and pushes me toward the door. "You go do what you need to, and then we'll meet back downstairs and wait on him to call me back."

"Stay with him," I whisper to Nathaniel on my way out.

It only takes me a few minutes to find the family and convince them to move on.

I promise their mother I will find out who did this to her husband, and it's one promise I intend to keep.

I wanted to go as a zombie, but Mary refused to let me. She said she was already going as a zombie nurse, so I had to pick something else. Halloween has never been my thing. But then again, I never really got to dress up and go trick or treating either. Costumes cost money, and my foster homes weren't going to shell out that kind of cash. Not that all of them were bad, just most of them.

What I end up wearing is an angel costume. Ironic, I know. It's cute, though, a short white dress, wings, and a fake halo. I'm wearing white stockings and blood red heels. Before the night is over, I'm going to fall and break my neck. If it hadn't been for Dan picking us up, I might have just washed my hands of the whole thing.

Eric invited us to his frat's Halloween party, and Mary insisted we go, saying we need to get out and socialize more. While I'm thrilled she's finally getting back into normal mode, I don't socialize. I never have, never will. The idea of a party where grown people are dressed up and so drunk they puke on the lawn is not my idea of fun.

Dan wraps an arm around me as soon as I get out of the car. He knows I'm clumsy and will likely end up in the ER if he doesn't keep me upright. He came dressed as Captain Jack Sparrow. Now, he's not Johnny Depp. Really, who could be Captain Jack but Johnny? But Dan does a good job of filling out the costume. He's even let his beard grow in a little so he has the dark scuff along his jaw and chin. It's made kissing him a whole new experience. I like the scruff. He looks older, sexier. I even told him I liked it, and he laughed, saying he may keep the look for a while.

The loud music is thumping before we even reach the house. I can hear the laughter, the catcalls, the general party festivity. It's been a long time since I went to a party. The one at the mill back in Charlotte, the night Sally died, was the last one I'd been to. Years. I guess Mary is right. After everything that's happened to us, we need to let loose a little and have some fun.

Eric is in the middle of everything, dressed like a mobster from the thirties. He looks adorable. When he sees us, a smile flashes across his lips. His date, some blonde with breasts too big to be real, pouts. Not one of those. I hate women who are clingy. She looks downright hostile when he lets go of her and jogs over to us.

"Hathaway, you do have a weird sense of humor."

I give him a cheeky grin. "You look dashing."

"I know it." Eric has always been a flirt and well aware of how gorgeous he is, both the old Eric and the new one in

Jake's body. Jake wasn't bad to begin with either, but with Eric in there now, he seems that much more.

"Where's the booze?" someone shouts from the door, and I look over to see Wade, the head of The Ghost Chasers, come through the door, followed by his cameraman, Ethan Cooper. We all notice the way Eric's entire body shifts in that direction, and it's not because of Wade. No one is pushing him, though. He has to figure this out on his own. I made sure to talk to Mary. Eric likes Ethan the way he's so desperately trying to like girls. Not that he doesn't like girls. He does, but he just likes Ethan a little more.

Over the last couple weeks, they've been hanging out and have become fast friends. It could be more, but unless it's something they're both willing to admit, it won't work.

I couldn't care less who Eric loves as long as he's happy. He just needs to get out of his own way and listen to his heart.

Hopefully, it'll come sooner rather than later.

Eric jerks his thumb behind him.

"Beer's in the kitchen!"

"Come on." Dan tugs me toward the sliding glass doors that lead out back, and I follow him. It's not any quieter out here with the music thumping, but at least it's not as crowded.

We end up in the back corner of the porch, with me leaning against the house and Dan pressed right up against me. "You want to leave?"

"What? We just got here."

He smiles lazily. "I know we just got here, but I know you well enough to know you hate this. Besides, our flight to Charlotte leaves at eight in the morning. We need an early night."

Lord knows I need all the extra strength I can get to deal with his mother.

"I'm not that much of a party person. Never was, really. I only did it to make sure I was in the 'in' crowd so no one could guess how weird I was."

"Do you know what kind of party I love?"

"What?"

"One with me, you, the couch, a good horror movie, and the lights down low.

All I need is you."

Melt my heart.

"What about Mary?"

"Eric can take her home."

He doesn't need to argue me into it. We find them both before ducking out and head back to Dan's hotel room. He really needs to get an apartment, but he wanted to wait until after the trial. No point in paying rent when he'll be gone for a good two to three weeks before the verdict is handed down.

He's moved hotels to a nicer one with room service. My dad offered to let him stay with him, but Dan refused. I wasn't surprised. Dan respects the fact Zeke is my father, but he doesn't like him. The cop in him rebels against everything my father stands for.

I don't hold it against him.

We stop at the Taco Bell drive-through and load up on food before heading back to the hotel. The closer we get, the more nervous I become. Dan and I have been dancing around each other since the day we met, and I think the dance is finally ending. Maybe tonight, maybe not.

He sets the bags down on the small table that serves as a desk and kicks off his shoes. "I got orange juice and Coke in the mini fridge. Can you find something to watch while I make a call? I need to check in with my dad."

"Sure." All but ripping the danged heels off, I find the remote and start flipping through channels. A *Halloween* marathon is just starting, so I settle on that. It's the old John Carpenter ones, way better than the remakes. I dig out two cans of Coke and find some paper plates before taking the food and jumping up on the bed.

Hey, the couch doesn't face the TV. The bed does. The smell of rich taco seasoning tickles my nose, and my stomach lets out a loud, appreciative sound. Even without the roogie curse, my stomach is a bottomless pit. I hope my metabolism never slows down, or I'm going to be in trouble.

My phone chirps, and I groan. I'd just gotten comfortable, dang it.

Getting up, I see a missed text from Cass. He wants to know if I'm up for hunting next week. They got a job in Memphis that needs a few more people. I text him to say no, I have to be in Charlotte next week. He probably forgot. In all honestly, I'm surprised Cass didn't denounce me when he found out I'm half demon. He thought about it for a few days and then came to see me. He apologized for how he reacted. He told me I'd more than proved I wasn't a demon, and he'd be glad to have me around for any hunts.

That meant a lot to me, especially after Eli's rejection. He'd gotten up and walked away, breaking my heart in the process. Dan had been there to pick it up and put it back together. Thinking back on everything now, there's never been any other choice for me. Dan accepts me for who I am. Always has and always will. He's it for me.

I will be glad to see Dan's dad, though. Earl Richards loves me like his own daughter, and I love him. I do have a proposal for him and Cameron, Dan's brother. His family means a lot to him, and I'm hoping they'll say yes.

The one thing I've discovered since working with Cass is that hunters don't have any real resources. They survive by the skin of their teeth, going into dangerous situations with little to no backup and substandard weapons. I want to change all that. Zeke gave me the green light to set up a foundation for the hunters, one where they can come and find the resources they need, where we can coordinate our efforts. I'm also going to talk to James Malone about helping to set us up with police departments across the country as consultants, so we are called in instead of trying to find ways to work around local law enforcement. If we can get access to what the cops know, it's better for everyone. Not sure that can be pulled off, but I'm going to try.

I want us all to be safe, but at the same time, as Zeke pointed out, that costs money. He's willing to donate a good chunk of the initial funding, but we need to find ways to earn cash and pay the hunters if we can. We definitely need to pay the staff that will run the day-to-day of the place.

Eric has come up with some great ideas on how to earn legitimate income. Some of them are good, some I'm not too sure about. He wants to start charging for ghostbusting services. Whereas most can't get rid of ghosts, I can. He says that's got to be worth something to rich people who want to keep things hush-hush. Maybe it'll work, maybe it won't. Either way, he's psyched.

I'm not good with handling large sums of money. My debit card gives me hives, so we'll need an accountant, and I'm hoping Dan's brother will take the job. And for legal counsel, who better than Earl Richards? He knows about the supernatural world, and he can help us set up the foundation and represent us where we need it. I'm guessing we're going to need it too. If it hadn't been for Cass and his clean-up crew, Dan, Nathaniel, and I would have been arrested at the Montgomery house.

I don't know what they did with the body, but Cass was right in that we couldn't let it be found. It would raise too many questions. He got rid of it. The swamp would be the easiest place to dump a body. Gators would have it eaten before daybreak.

And I haven't forgotten my promise either. I will track down the person who cursed Mr. Montgomery and make them pay for the lives they stole. Zeke is working on it, and as soon as we have a lead, I'm there.

Dan looks extremely tired when he comes back inside. I know everything with his mom is wearing him down. He's torn up inside over it, and all I can do is be there for him, and I don't try to tell him everything will be okay. That would be a lie, and we made a promise to never hide anything from each other again.

I even let Silas remove the buffer he'd used to mute the worst of my feelings from Dan. Well, "let" would be a figurative term. He'd kept me for three days, repairing all the tattoos and sigils, muttering about ripping my stomach out through my nose while it growled. He was furious when he saw the mess the roogies's claws had made. Rhea might have healed the wounds, but she didn't fix the tats. That was all Silas.

I did talk to him about the locked door she'd found. Just like Rhea, his face paled and he went into a rage, snarling and throwing things. I tried to leave, but he snatched me back and forced me downstairs where he could work on my tats without fear of anyone else seeing what he was doing. The thought of a god setting me up to get hurt didn't sit well with him. It scared him more than even Deleriel did. Never a good sign.

"Everything good with your dad?" I open the bags and start unloading tacos onto the plates.

"Yeah." Dan palms his neck and rubs at it. "He's just stressed."

"I bet. Here." I hold his plate out to him. "Come eat. You'll feel better."

He stops at the fridge and pulls out a beer instead of the Coke I'd gotten him. He doesn't drink often, but I'm not going to begrudge him one tonight. Not with everything coming up next week.

He jumps on the bed, slightly bouncing the food bags. "Thanks, Squirt."

"You got it, Officer Dan." I motion to

the TV. "*Halloween* marathon good?"

"I loved these movies as a kid. Michael Myers scared the crap out of me." He shoves almost half of an entire taco in his mouth, and I scrunch up my nose. I may have a bottomless pit of a stomach, but I take the time to chew.

"You are so gross."

"You love me anyway."

Shaking my head, I pick up my own taco and sit back to watch the movie. A little while later, and several belches, the food is gone, and it's just the two of us snuggled up together, watching Michael stalk all the teenagers.

"What if they convict her?"

"Then they do."

"Part of me wants them to find her guilty," he confesses.

Ah, here is what's been weighing him down. The cop in him, his sense of right and wrong, that's what's been eating him alive. He loves her, but he knows she's guilty, and that needs to be punished. The sword he holds only makes it worse.

"That's because you know the difference between right and wrong, but it doesn't mean you don't love her."

"What if she gets off? How is that right? Amelia and the Malones get no justice."

I sit up and straddle his lap so I can take his face into my hands. "You can't control what happens in that courtroom. It's up to a jury to find her guilty or innocent. Both sides will lay out their cases, and then they'll render a verdict. No matter what happens, she'll still be your mother, and you'll still love her. That will never change. We will accept what happens and move on. It's all we can do."

Instead of saying a word, he leans forward and kisses me.

Just like the first time he kissed me, it's not instant fireworks. It's a slow burn that starts in the pit of my stomach and spirals outward, consuming everything until there's nothing but a blazing heat that overwhelms and drowns out every sensation. I've felt fireworks, I've felt butterflies, but none of that comes close to what I feel when Dan kisses me.

He is my home.

"I love you," he whispers when he manages to pull his lips from mine. "I love you so much, Mattie Louise Hathaway. You know, that right?"

"I do."

"Remember what I told you when we go back to Charlotte. She's going to try everything to run you off. I know it. Don't let her."

"No one's running me off. I promise. I'm in it for the long haul, same as you." I take a deep breath and lean my forehead against his so all I can see is the warm chocolate color of his eyes. "Now, why don't we forget about tomorrow, forget about the trial, forget about hunters and demons and gods, and just focus on you and me? For tonight, let's just be Dan and Mattie."

"I can do that."

"Then show me how much you love me, Dan." I lean in and kiss the bridge of his nose. "Show me."

He sucks in a breath, realizing what I'm asking. "You sure?"

"I've never been surer of anything in my entire life."

After that, there are no words, but then words aren't required.

Tomorrow, we'll deal with the storm brewing, but for tonight, it's just me and Officer Dan.

For once, all in my life is right.

Even if it only lasts for a night.

Want to know what's happening with Mattie and Dan and ask all the questions you have?
Then join Apryl's Reading Group!
https://www.facebook.com/groups/AprylsAngels/

ACKNOWLEDGEMENTS

I have stressed so much in moving these characters out of young adult and into college and adulthood where they will deal with more mature themes, but Mattie can't be a kid forever. She has to grow up, and I hope I am pacing that well. Those of you who have sat and listened to me fret over this for hours, thank you. Just being there helps me, and for that, I'm grateful.

I know some will be angry at me for moving this series into adulthood, but it's necessary for Mattie to grow into the young woman she will become, for her to be the hunter she needs to be. I hope you give the new Mattie a chance. She's still the same foster kid at heart, but she's learning to be more than that, to be who she was meant to be. She's finding her own way and making mistakes and finding everything she needs to make her happy. It's going to be a wild couple of books getting her there. So, I ask that you please take the ride with me.

As always, thanks to Limitless Publishing for believing in Mattie when no one else would. Thank y'all so much.

My editor, Lori Whitwam, you've taught me so much, and you put up with my yoyoing schedule. I think I'd cry if you quit on me and I had to find a new editor ☺

For my family and friends who put up with me going dark for days while I work. You all know I love you even when I'm a hermit.

Mostly, though, thanks to all the fans out there who made *The Ghost Files* the international phenomenon it became and continue to support it through its re-emergence as *The Crane Diaries*. Your support keeps me writing, and as long as even one person is entertained by nonsense, I will keep writing.

Thank you all so much!

All my love,
Apryl Baker